3RD TANGO

SCHOCK SISTERS MYSTERY SERIES, BOOK 3

MISTY EVANS
ADRIENNE GIORDANO

3rd Tango, Schock Sisters Mystery Series, Book 3

Copyright © 2019 Misty Evans & Adrienne Giordano

ISBN Print: 978-1-942504-38-2

Publisher: ALG Publishing, LLC

Cover Art by Fanderclai Design

Formatting by Beach Path Publishing, LLC

Editing by Gina Bernal, Elizabeth Neal, Patricia Essex

Please Note

ACKNOWLEDGMENTS

As usual, a huge thanks to John Leach, our law enforcement go-to guy when it comes to getting our characters in and out of trouble.

Thanks also to Gina Bernal, Elizabeth Neal, Patricia Essex, Sam Fanderclai, Leiha Mann, Liz Semkiu and Amy Remus for your continued support. You are an awesome team!

To our families, thank you, thank you, thank you for all that you do to help us on this wild ride that is a writing career.

1

Charlie

Sunday dinners are something I always look forward to with my parents. Until today.

Dad's heading out for a fishing trip with his friends, so Mom switched it to Saturday lunch and topped it off by insisting Meg and I bring our boyfriends.

I'm honestly not sure I want JJ to meet them. Yet.

Our relationship is just starting to deepen, and well, my parents can be a handful.

The summer is in full-swing, the temperature pushing the low nineties. D.C. is swamped in humidity and sunshine. "There are three subjects you do not want to bring up or engage in," I tell JJ Carrington III and Jerome Metcalfe. I hold up a finger. "One, politics."

In the backseat, Meg expands on this to Jerome. "Dad gets hot under the collar about the state of the economy, healthcare, and just about everything else related to Washington."

"Two," I hold up another and spear Jerome with a look in the rearview as I take the offramp from the highway, heading southwest. "Legalized marijuana."

Meg's boyfriend deals in the stuff, along with being a brilliant artist, and talks as casually about it as I would breakfast.

Once more Meg chimes in. "Mom is for it, Dad isn't. Funny too, since they grew up during the sixties. Charlie and I are pretty sure they experimented with pot at least a few times."

In the passenger seat, JJ laughs softly under his breath. He looks and smells good enough to eat, and I smile when he glances at me with his beautiful blue-gray eyes. My dad will love him—he's an alpha male, a U.S. District Attorney, and treats me like a queen. His recovery after being shot at my place several months ago has gone well, and I thank the universe for him every day. It was my fault he nearly died. I'll never take him—or any of my family—for granted again.

"And three," I continue, "do not bring up anything about serial killers or the neighbors."

Both men give me odd looks. My sister fills them in about this as well. "Mom's sure the man across the street is not just eccentric, but a serial killer and she spent the majority of our youth trying to prove it."

Meg and I run a private investigation service, and it's only been a few months since our run-in with a legitimate serial killer, so it's been a frequent topic of conversation. Today, the last thing I want to talk about is work, though things are good right now. However, it's unavoidable as either Mom or Dad will surely bring it up. After our last two prominent cases in the public eye, we came out looking competent and successful, although it was rocky on the most recent. Business is up enough that I'm considering hiring another junior investigator to help. Expansion is something Meg and I have been discussing off and on for a while now.

"Whoa," Jerome says, his honey-blond hair is in a low bun

and he has removed the earring. He's clean shaven and wearing a nice polo shirt and khaki pants—somewhat of an upgrade from his usual artistic, pot-dealing self. "That must have been freaky."

Meg leans her shoulder against his, and I see the love in her eyes. "Mom was an investigative reporter until she gave it up to stay home with us. Dad was gone a lot, being career Army. Her brain needed something besides dirty diapers and endless rounds of Chutes and Ladders. The guy was always a touch suspicious acting, but she does have an overactive imagination, to say the least."

We arrive, and after I park and get out of the car, JJ takes my hand as we stroll to the door. "Stop worrying," he says. "It's just lunch."

He doesn't realize he's about to walk into a gauntlet of my father's endless questions and my mother's need to find something wrong with him and Jerome.

I envy Meg—she doesn't seem nervous at all. She and Jerome laugh and talk as they climb the steps of the back porch. JJ stops me at the bottom and bends to kiss my forehead. "I promise to be on my best behavior."

"I'm not worried about you. It's them I'm worried about."

He puts an arm around me and we climb the stairs together.

Mom greets us and ushers us into the kitchen, her and Dad shaking hands with Jerome and JJ, Mom hugging Meg and kissing my cheek.

Light conversation follows as we seat our boyfriends at the dining room table and Dad takes his spot at the head of it. Meg and I already worked this out. I stay there to referee the conversation, while she helps Mom bring in the food.

Everything goes well, the dishes are passed around, both guests making complimentary comments about the house and the different items Mom made. It is an impressive spread. She never seemed interested in cooking when Meg and I were

young, and many of our meals consisted of Cheerios and mac and cheese. In recent years, she's become quite a foodie. Everything in front of us is homemade, some of it organic, and most requiring more than three ingredients—something Mom never tackled before.

There's general conversation regarding the weather and heat—we haven't had rain in weeks, and everyone is weary of all the sunshine and humidity.

JJ asks about the family homestead and Dad fills him in, proud of his father and grandfather, the two generations who lived here before him. He also throws in a little zinger about how he hopes Meg or I might move in when he and Mom are gone. I suppress an eye roll as this subject seems to come up more and more as they age. As if they're both going to up and disappear on us at the same time.

Meg and I exchange a glance across the table, her slight brow lift my cue to redirect the conversation. "How's your golf game, Dad?"

I know very well how it is—he pretty much stinks—but he likes to talk about it and the details regarding his latest outing with a group of fellow retired, veteran friends.

This is a safe, although slightly boring, topic, that allows the rest of us to eat. He moves onto his upcoming trip, and yep, I relish the fact that everyone I love is safe, and the biggest thing we all have to discuss is lures, fishing poles, and trips.

Mom interjects and turns to JJ. "What do your initials stand for?"

He swallows and dabs the napkin to his lips. "Joseph Jefferson. I was named after my grandfathers."

Dad makes an approving noise. "Joseph Jefferson Carrington, the third. Sounds like a strong presidential candidate."

Dad winks at me while cutting the meat on his plate and loading his fork. "Ever think of running for office?"

JJ takes a drink of iced tea. Buying time? "Not high on my list of priorities, but it's not off the table."

This makes my father extremely happy, while I turn a raised eyebrow on my boyfriend. "You never told me that."

He gives a deprecating smile. "I like to keep my options open."

I'm truly stunned. With a "hmm," I signify we'll discuss this more later.

Mother turns to Jerome. "Meg mentioned the other day you're thinking of moving. This is a lovely residential area, and I know the Petersons on the next block are putting their condo up for sale. Ask Meg, it's a great place for artists. We're one of the few neighborhoods left with woods so nearby. You like to connect with nature, I bet. I know Meg does."

Her hint is obvious, and I try not to laugh, thinking about Jerome, who can barely match clothes or remember when he's supposed to pick Meg up, buying a condo in this neighborhood.

"I'll have to check it out," he says, and Meg smiles. She knows as well as I that he has no intention of doing so, realizing he'd be far too close to our parents for one thing, as well as out of his price range in this area. Hell, I doubt JJ could afford it. The only reason my parents are here is the generational inheritance.

"It's too bad we can't get the neighbor across the street to move," Mom says in a disgusted voice. "I'm getting closer, though. It won't be long until I'll have enough for the police to arrest him."

Meg kicks me under the table. Here we go.

Lunch was going so well, and now I have to find a way to divert Mom off the subject we feared would come up. A tense silence falls from JJ and Jerome, the two knowing we just dove head first into the hot zone.

Dad puts down his fork with a clank. "Helen, not now."

Mom looks around, wide-eyed and innocent. "What? I'm just saying, the man is going to jail. I'll make certain of it. Of course, who'd want that house, knowing a serial killer lived in it."

She totally believes this is the truth. At the continued silence, she straightens her spine. "I'm working with the CSCC." She nods at Meg and I, as if this makes sense to us. "We're compiling all the evidence we can find linking Gayle to at least three cold case deaths. My notes from all these years are key to proving he's been getting away with murder." She leans forward and lowers her voice. "Literally."

JJ digs into his mashed potatoes. "CSCC?"

I pinch him under the table for engaging the enemy, as Mom nods adamantly. "Citizens Solving Cold Cases. The group has grown considerably in the last year, and we've had success with more than six cases. You should join," she says to him. "We have former police officers, detectives, even a retired FBI agent. He founded it." At this, she flicks her eyes to me. "We could use people like you helping us."

Meg kicks me again, and I give her a look telling her I don't know how to change this flow of conversation. "Mom, can we talk about this later? Tell us what you made for dessert."

She screws up her face, letting me know she's not going to be diverted. She rises from the chair and walks out of the room. Meg and I glance at Dad.

He shakes his head, as conflicted about what to say as we are. He tosses his napkin on the table and stands. "I'll check on dessert."

Before he steps away, Mom strides in, arms loaded with blue file folders. She *thunks* the stack next to my plate, making the silverware jump. "No one move. Here are my notes, and the recent internet investigation Al conducted with my guidance."

I look up to see determination and something else brewing behind her brown eyes—the investigative reporter she was in

6

her heyday. "I'd love to go through these after lunch. It's great that you've joined a group." Total lie. That's the last thing she needs, other people encouraging and supporting her obsession with our neighbor.

"Who's Al?" Jerome asks, and I see Meg turn her fierce gaze on him.

"Alfonzo Baez," Mom answers. "The retired agent I mentioned. He and I were going through my notes from the mid-nineties, and he saw a link between information I had on Gayle, our neighbor, and a place in Virginia he knew about where three women's bodies turned up in the early 2000s."

Now that, as much as I hate it, catches my interest.

"The fishing cabins on Whitetop?" Dad asks.

The mountain is a popular spot with hikers, hunters, and fishing enthusiasts. Mom nods and points at him, like we're playing charades and he's guessed right. "Remember the weekend you took me up there? We went without the girls, so we could have some alone time, and I thought I saw Gayle's car at another cabin on that lane?" Mom turns back to me. "Your father wouldn't let me go say hi, but when we got home, Gayle was putting the garbage out. I told him I thought I saw him there and he threatened me."

Her face is flushed and she's shaking slightly with anger. I've never heard this story and I glance at Meg, questioningly and she shakes her head.

"You never told me that," Dad says, and I can see he's now angry at Gayle. Dad is extremely protective of all of us. "Why, that no good bastard. I ought to walk over there and knock his block off!"

Perfect. Could this spin any farther out of control? I jump to my feet, ready to intercept him, even though I feel like confronting Gayle myself. "Let's take a deep breath." I turn to Mom. "How exactly did he threaten you?"

"Told me I was a nosy bitch and needed to leave him alone.

He went to the woods to get away from everybody, especially his snoopy neighbor. Said he knew I was always watching him, and if I didn't stop, he'd get a restraining order."

"Mom," Meg says, sounding astonished. "What if he is a killer? You could've been in serious danger."

She waves this off. "I had my can of pepper spray, and your father was within shouting distance. That's not the point." Another tap of the files. "Last week, I was telling Al about the run-in and he remembered that bodies were discovered buried in that location, and now he has Gayle linked to that area, thanks to my research."

Okay. That is something, even though it's still circumstantial. Mostly, I'm relieved she didn't end up with the other bodies.

"You never should have confronted him," Dad chastises. "Not without me there to look out for you."

Wrong thing to say. "I took care of myself and your daughters just fine while you were traveling all over the world. Gave up my career for yours. I think we did just fine."

She looks at me and nods, encouraging me to support this declaration.

It is true, but I still hold out hope of salvaging our lunch. "You know what? I'm sure Al and his group can continue to assist you in your investigation. Meanwhile, I'd like to finish our meal and talk about something less depressing."

She slams a hand on top of the folders. "There's a man next door who's been murdering young girls for *years* and no one's done a damn thing about it."

That's because there isn't any actual proof. I've had this argument with her many times, and yet, there's no winning it. Still, this development with the bodies has me curious. I may have to look into it on the downlow while I try to distance my mother from it.

I set my hand on top of hers. "You're an amazing investiga-

tor, and I'm sure that's where Meg and I inherited our skills," I attempt to placate her, "but this is the first time JJ and Jerome have had a chance to meet you and Dad. I'm sure they'd prefer to discuss less gruesome things over their food. Let's get back to something normal."

Please, I mentally plead.

"Well, guess what? I'm tired of everyone acting like I'm crazy. I'll make you a deal, Charlize."

I know I shouldn't ask, but what else can I do? "Okay, Mom." I start to pick up the folders, attempting to take this on alone so the others can resume eating. "How about we go in the other room and talk about this deal?"

She won't take her hand off the stack, pressing down and not allowing me to cart the folders off. "I know I'm right. If it's the last thing I do, I'll prove Gayle Morton is a serial killer, and you're going to help me."

At this point, I simply have to agree in order to pacify her. "Okay, Mom. What can I do?"

"Good." The tension in her face relaxes slightly. She taps the files. "I want to hire you and your sister."

"What?"

She nods and smiles. "I'm done playing around. I'm hiring Schock Investigations to help me prove our neighbor is a serial killer."

9

2

Meg

I've known for a while now my mother is nuts.

The odd part is that neither I nor any of my family members find this to be a big deal. It's simply the way it is. An accepted part of life. Charlie likes designer shoes, I enjoy micro-dosing weed and Dad loves genealogy.

Mom?

Crazy.

Typical American family.

Except, according to my mother, we have a serial killer across the street. And after this latest news about the three bodies found on Whitetop, I'm beginning to think she isn't as wacko as we thought. In her day, she was an excellent journalist. Something, in recent years, I've tended to not give her enough credit for.

I swing my head to Jerome who stares at the prongs of his

fork as if they've suddenly sprouted wings. Smart man staying out of this one. Across from me, JJ uses his cloth napkin to hide a smile. Our esteemed United States Attorney for the District of Columbia is amused.

By a serial killer.

Talk about twisted.

His sense of humor is one of the things that binds him and Charlie. Without a doubt, it's a coping mechanism that keeps them emotionally stable while investigating cases involving child molesters, rapists, and murderers.

"Mom," Charlie says, "we should take this into the other room."

As if that'll work? My sister should know better.

Mom lets out a huff and waves a manicured hand at JJ. Mom, like Charlie, is big on personal grooming. With their sculpted cheeks and slim builds, they're knockouts.

"We have JJ here," Mom says. "He can help."

At that, JJ lets out a noise that might be a half cough-half gag.

The hot-shot lawyer isn't laughing now.

"Yes." I give him a rueful smile. "JJ can."

He spears me with a look and my smile widens. If he intends to be part of this family, he needs to embrace the chaos.

Join the ranks like the rest of us.

"No," Charlie says. "He can't. At least not until we have solid evidence."

At the end of the table, Dad grabs his and Mom's empty plates and once again rises, this time appearing more determined to make his getaway. "I'll take JJ and Jerome out back. Show them the new shed."

The new shed.

Lamest excuse ever, but Jerome and JJ—weaklings that they are—bolt from their seats, quickly stacking dishes as they go.

Charlie shakes her head. "Cowards."

Clearly unfazed, the men keep moving. It's just as well. This is Jerome's first meeting with my parents and I'd prefer to ease him in. If that's even possible after this episode.

Mom slides back into her chair and waves us over. "Come sit by me. I know once you see what I have, you'll understand."

I doubt it, but if it'll get her out of this obsession once and for all, I think we'll need to suck it up.

"All right." Charlie sits next to her. "Let's see what you have. But I'm not promising anything."

Surprisingly, Mom nods. "I have no problem with that. Believe me, you'll want in on this."

Mom removes a folder from the top and slides the rest to the center of the table. "This is my most recent research."

She flips it open and—pfft—smacks pages of typed notes on the table. I lean in to peruse the first document and let out a low whistle.

My mother, given her history as a reporter, is no slouch when it comes to surveillance. Outlined in front of us, broken down by day and hour, is one week of Gayle's activities. Mom is nothing if not thorough and her notes prove it.

"Lord, Mom," Charlie says. "You're keeping daily tabs on the man."

"Well, of course. How else am I supposed to gather evidence?"

She has a point there. I move to page two. Tuesday's activities. At nine in the morning, Gayle dragged his garbage cans and recycling bin to the curb, adding a desk chair that, according to the notes, appeared to have a broken arm.

Twenty minutes later, he drove off in his ten-year-old Toyota, returning at ten-oh-three with a woman.

Forgetting that I should be horrified my mother is spending her days sitting in a window spying on her neighbor, I key in on Gayle's guest.

"Who's the woman?"

"His girlfriend."

Charlie meets Mom's eye. "You know this for sure?"

"Well, she's there a lot and spends the night. I think she's living there. Until five months ago, I'd never seen her before. Unless it's his long-lost sister, I'm going with girlfriend. I think she's an artist."

This little detail interests me. "What makes you think that?"

Half-rising, Mom rifles through the stack, withdrawing one halfway down.

She holds it up. "Garage sale last month. I wandered over there."

Charlie's mouth drops open. "Mom, seriously? You're convinced he's a murderer and you walked over there? You just told us he threatened you all those years ago. Where was Dad?"

"He was putting the shed together. He doesn't know I went."

My sister leans forward, looking straight at me. "Am I the only one that thinks it's a little wacky she did that?"

I wave a hand over the documents laid before us. The whole damn thing is firmly entrenched in Screwyville. Why should snooping in a suspected serial killer's household items be a problem?

"Right," Charlie says, obviously understanding my point. "What was there?"

"Nothing special. Lamps, dishes, the normal stuff."

"No bloody axes?"

Mom, clearly unhappy with my humor, pins me with a look. "Hardy, har, smarty pants. If you're not going to take this seriously, I'll find someone else. I've worked hard and you're... minimizing...it. I don't appreciate that, Megan."

The use of my given name indicates her distaste. Shame burns my throat. No matter how off-base I think this whole thing is, she's a smart woman who believes our neighbor is a murderer. For that alone, I need to respect what she's accomplished.

I hold up my hands. "I'm sorry. You're right."

I take the folder, set it on the table and flip it open. More hyper-detailed notes of Gayle and the woman's activities and a full inventory—with photos—of their garage sale items.

At this point, I don't know what to hope for. If he winds up being just a quirky neighbor, my mother will have spent what equates to years of her life surveilling him. All that time. Lost.

She will, in short, be devastated if a serial killer doesn't live across the street.

How the hell did we get here?

Sighing, I skim the list of catalogued items. Midway down I pause.

"Art supplies?"

"I knew you'd like that," Mom says. "She had brushes, canvasses, graphite pencils, the works. There was a nice easel I thought you might like, but I refrained."

Now my mother is pushing it and the urge to wisecrack terrorizes me.

No, no, no. Nope. Not doing it.

I gnaw on my lip. Later, I'll tell Charlie I want serious bonus points for not cracking a joke about our mom buying art supplies from a murderer.

I flip to the next page where a flyer announces a neighboring town's upcoming festival.

"What's this?"

Mom taps her finger against it. "I picked it up from the table with all the art supplies. I didn't ask, but I heard his girlfriend tell one of their customers she'll have a booth. I'm assuming she'll be selling her art. If that's what she wants to call it." Mom shudders. "She's no match for my Meg, that's for sure."

Aww, thanks, Mom.

Charlie leans in again. "When is it?"

I check the flyer. "This weekend."

"Oh, hell."

I meet Charlie's eye and know exactly what she's thinking. The festival? Total catnip when it comes to surveilling a target. If I know my sister at all, we'll be hunting down Gayle and the mystery woman and possibly buying some art.

3

Charlie

*S*unday morning I'm at my desk fanning myself with a piece of paper.

It's only ten, but the heat index is nearly a hundred outside and I have the feeling our air-conditioning is on its last leg. I need to wrap up at least one of the three cases on my desk so we can get paid. Since I'd like to stay as cool as possible, I'm debating whether I can hand off the case requiring leg work to Matt, so I can stay in the office.

My phone pings, the security app alerting me I have company. The camera over the back door shows Meg arriving, dressed in shorts and a tank top, a wide brimmed hat in her hands. She uses her key, resets the system, and stops in my doorway a few moments later. "What are you doing?"

"I'm working." I wave a hand across the stack of files, making it obvious. "Since I couldn't get everything done yesterday due to our fabulous lunch."

"We're supposed meet Mom in twenty minutes."

I don't have to tell my sister that going to an art festival with our mother, in order to snoop on Gayle and his girlfriend, ranks right up there with my worst nightmare.

"Art festivals are your territory. I have three clients whose cases I should wrap up this weekend, so I'm staying here. You go with Mom."

She leans a shoulder against the doorjamb and gives me a scorching glare. "You promised to help with this investigation."

I point to the stack of folders she gave us at the most-embarrassing-lunch-in-recent-history, sitting on the credenza behind me. "I've been working my way through all of those files, but these cases hired us first, and they don't get the family discount."

"She's our mother."

The word conveys so much more than your everyday label. Familial loyalty, our mom's ferocity when it came to raising us, her undying love and protection.

"I know that, and I'm taking it seriously, I promise. I've made an appointment with this Al Baez guy to discuss the case with him at three. I want to know more about the three bodies found in the Whitetop Mountain woods."

Meg gives me a look that says that's not good enough and she's dragging me with them, regardless, when another alert lets me know someone's at the back door.

I raise a finger, pausing the chastising speech she's about to launch into, and check my phone for the video feed. "It's JJ. What's he doing here?"

He peers up at the camera, smiling. He's dressed in casual clothes and sunglasses.

I buzz him in, hoping he can help get me out of this shindig. Maybe he's bringing me a new case from the District Attorney's office. Not that I want more work, or that we need it, but anything to keep me from having to poke my eyes out at the festival.

Meg launches into her argument, and I sit there and take it. She chews me out about not taking Mom more seriously, about how she was an accomplished journalist, not to mention the only mother we'll ever have, etc., laying the guilt on with an extra dose.

"Meg, you know I can't imagine what our life would be without her, and I respect her for giving up her career to raise us while Dad was gone. I made peace a long time ago with her obsession over Gayle, but honestly, it's unhealthy, and you and I both have legitimate cases. I'm not blowing this off. I *am* going to meet with her friend from the CSCC. If there's any tie between Gayle and these bodies, and this guy feels I should dig deeper, I'll do it."

JJ appears behind Meg. He lifts a hand in greeting as she half-turns toward him. "Are we ready?"

"For what?" I ask, feeling my hopes sinking.

He looks confused, glancing between us. "We're supposed to be meeting your mom in a few minutes, aren't we?"

I throw my hands up and sit back in my chair. "Oh, for God's sake. You, too?"

He leans on the opposite doorjamb, his wide shoulder bumping Meg's petite one. He grins cheekily. "I have nothing better to do on this hot Sunday than spend time with three beautiful women."

I'm such a sucker for him. He always knows exactly what to say to throw me off guard and make me feel tingly inside.

Damn him.

Charlie Schock doesn't do tingly. I don't do art festivals. "You and Meg run along," I tell him, but I feel my resolve slipping. "Tell Mom I said hi, and I'm meeting with her friend. That will make her happy."

The back door buzzes again, and I glance over to see... "Oh no."

Meg comes forward to glance at my screen. "What?"

She groans. I hit the buzzer so the door will unlock, and seconds later, Mom's voice rings out. "Hello. I'm here. Where are you guys?"

Meg meets my eyes. Her voice is a whisper. "What is she doing here?"

JJ moves aside as Mom sweeps into the room. "Good morning. Are you all ready to go?"

"I thought we were meeting you there," Meg says.

Mom is dressed in a linen outfit, a gauzy scarf around her neck, dark sunglasses and a straw hat. She has an extra hat in hand. "I thought we should get our undercover story straight before we go."

She glances at me. "Charlize, is that what you're wearing?"

I'm dressed in my usual white shirt and dark pants. I glance at myself, wondering exactly what she thought I should wear.

With a frown, she pivots back to Meg. "So who are we pretending to be? What if Gayle is there? Do you think he'll be pissy again, if he recognizes me? Do you want me to hang back so the gal doesn't?"

I feel a headache forming between my temples. "You're not undercover, Mom. This is not a spy mission."

Meg laughs. "We're going as ourselves, but you should stay out of sight, just in case Gayle is there. Charlie will ask his girlfriend some questions, see if she gets any clues, while I look at her art."

Mom looks disappointed.

I stand and text Matt about the case I'm dumping on him. He'll be okay with it—he needs money to pay off the giant diamond he just bought his new fiancée.

"I'm not going anywhere near the art festival. I have work that has to get done today." At Mom's hard look, I continue, "I'm meeting with your friend later. Baez? That's all the time I have for your case this weekend. First thing Monday, I'll dive in more fully. Hopefully, Baez has pertinent information on those bodies I can start with."

She worries the brim of the hat in her hands. Gives me puppy dog eyes. The accusation. The disappointment. "You can't spare a few hours to go with us? Please, Charlize. I so rarely get to spend time with you."

Meg and I have dinner with her and Dad every Sunday. She saw me at lunch yesterday, and spent the majority of the time talking about a suspected serial killer. Welcome to Guilt Town, USA. My mother is an expert hostess there. "It's not exactly like I can walk up to this woman and start asking questions about Gayle." I'm still trying to weasel out of this, but my resolve is crumbling. It's probably easier to get it over with and get back here as soon as possible. "What am I supposed to say, oh hey, is Gayle burying bodies in the backyard?"

Mom looks offended.

Meg snorts. She links an elbow with Mom's. "Charlie, you and JJ drive separately from us, and that way, you can return here once we check out this gal's booth. If the opportunity arises for one of us to ask her some questions, just friendly stuff, we'll take it. If not, no harm done. I'll help you finish those"—she points at my desk—"before the weekend is over. Win-win."

JJ, behind both of them, wiggles his fingers at me, a come-on gesture. "If there's anything I can do to help, I'll pitch in, too." He hammers the last nail in my coffin. "Come on, Charlize. A little fresh air will do you good."

Three against one. I'm a former FBI agent, trained in interrogation, manipulation, pressure. Normally, those odds don't bother me.

Today, maybe it's the heat, JJ's eyes, or my mother's flippin' guilt trip. I want to dig in my heels, but I can't seem to work up the effort.

I toss the pen I'm holding on top of the files. "Fine," I acquiesce. "I'll give you a couple hours, no more." I point to Meg, then JJ. "And you two are mine for the rest of the weekend."

"Deal," Meg says.

Behind her, JJ winks. "I think that's doable."

Mom hands me the hat in her hands. "You're going to need this," she says. "And I hope you have some dark sunglasses. This is going to be so fun!"

I sigh, pretty sure this will be a complete, and utter, disaster.

4

Meg

We're an interesting bunch. Charlie, myself, our mother, JJ and Jerome, are all wandering the festival. As expected, I lost Jerome three tents back after he got into a debate with a booth owner over hatching and smudging techniques.

It's probably just as well he's occupied. After all, six people in a group tend to stick out and with JJ looking like a GQ model, we don't exactly blend.

"JJ," I say, "not to be rude, but you need to hang back. You're like something off a romance novel cover."

Charlie nods her agreement. "She's right. We're trying to be low-key here and every woman we pass drools over you."

This causes him to unleash his flashing smile that, in his bachelor days, probably charmed the pants off countless women.

"No problem," he says. "I'll wait on Jerome."

His agreement doesn't shock me. The Emperor of Cold Cases isn't stupid. If this investigation turns into something, JJ's involvement could be called into question and none of us want a career ruined.

If JJ disappears for a few minutes while we do some good, old-fashioned reconnoitering, he has all sorts of plausible deniability.

He drops a quick kiss on Charlie's lips and disappears into the throng of people perusing stained glass assortments, sculptures, pottery and thousands of other handmade creations along the three-block route.

Our not-so-strategic plan is to surveil Marie Anderson, the girlfriend of our neighbor, then attempt to gather information on her. All without Mom being spotted. We've agreed it would be best if she doesn't appear to be too interested in Marie. The only problem is, Mom and Dad are the only ones who've met her and can point her out. And he's not here.

We've already knocked off one block without a Marie sighting. If she's here, she must be along the next two. We trudge on and the thick, humid air causes rivulets of sweat to drip from my neck, straight down my spine. Throw in all the people and I'm ready for air-conditioning.

Within the crush of bodies, Mom sticks to the middle of the street where she can view the booths on either side.

"Whoopsie," she says, cutting a sharp left in front of me, nearly knocking me off my feet.

I grab Charlie to regain my balance then let go before anyone notices me. "What?"

Mom jerks her head in the opposite direction. "That's her. The redhead talking to the man in the John Lennon sunglasses."

In her attempt to stay clear of Marie, Mom breaks for the booth two down from us.

"Finally," Charlie says. "It's so damned hot my cleavage is a

MISTY EVANS & ADRIENNE GIORDANO

swamp. Mom is losing her mind and since I'm here, I must be right there with her."

A swamp. Funny. A snort breaks free. "Once we check on Marie, we'll clear her and talk Mom out of this investigation."

Even I, who tends to support my mother on her endeavors, have to admit I find myself wishing she'd stuck to her career while Charlie and I were growing up. If she'd done that, maybe now she wouldn't be so desperate to feed her curiosity.

Or destroy the reputation of her quirky neighbor by accusing him of being a serial killer.

Oh, the tangled web.

I run a hand over my neck, then wipe the moisture on my jeans. "What's the plan?"

The thing about my former FBI agent sister is that she always has a plan. It might be an instantly-created one, but she never goes into a situation without an expectation of what she's looking for.

A woman wheeling a folding shopping cart half-filled with various items zig-zags between us and Charlie blows out a hard breath. "I hate these things. Too many people."

"Not to mention the swampy cleavage."

Charlie weaves through a couple with a stroller then bolts into a small but opportune opening in pedestrian traffic. "Keep up," she tells me as I dodge the flow wandering past Marie.

The man in the glasses takes a card from her, promising to contact her at a later date, which, I assume, translates to him passing on whichever painting they'd been discussing.

As Charlie closes in on our target, I take a second to study the landscapes lining the tent walls. Mostly watercolors, all are blends of similar colors. Burnt sienna, cobalt blue, yellow ochre and French ultramarine, abound. Marie's technique isn't bad, but a tendency to outline in dark colors gives the pieces a cut-out, amateurish look.

"Hello," Charlie says.

Marie smiles and I sense a willowy easiness in her that immediately puts me at ease. Artsy people. We have that gift. The dimple in her left cheek doesn't hurt.

She shifts her gaze to me. For a few seconds, she studies me with narrowed eyes and I nod, pointing at one of the watercolors. "I love this."

"Thank you. It's the George Washington bridge."

"Is that the Little Red Lighthouse?"

Wide-eyed surprise lights her face. "You know it? How wonderful."

As a kid, my mother would read me a children's book about the Little Red Lighthouse along Manhattan's Hudson River. To this day, it's my favorite.

Marie's gaze ping-pong's between Charlie and me. Something is up and my guess is she's trying to figure out if she knows us.

"We both do." Charlie eyes the painting. "It's lovely. What's the price?"

Okay. Lovely might be pushing it.

"Thank you. I paint them myself. That particular one is a hundred-and-twenty."

I nearly choke. Reconnoitering notwithstanding, if my sister pays over a hundred dollars, I'll kill her.

"Ooh," Charlie says. "That's out of my range."

Marie nods then glances back at me. "I'm sorry I'm staring, but I've seen you before. In my neighborhood." She points at Charlie. "You drive that nice car. You visit the people across the street."

And, we're busted. Nothing left to do now but roll with it. Pretend like it's no big deal. Charlie will probably kill me, but we're on a mission here. "They're our parents," I say. "I'm Meg Schock. This is my sister, Charlie. I'm an artist also. Our mother mentioned she saw your flyer about the art fair. We thought we'd check it out."

Marie huffs. "Your mother spies on us."

"Yes," Charlie agrees, raising her eyebrows at me then turning her attention to Marie. "Sorry about that. We heard about the run-in with Gayle. Mom doesn't mean any harm. She's...protective...of the neighborhood. Likes to keep an eye on things."

Marie's gaze bounces between us again and I do my best to look thoroughly repentant on behalf of our mother.

"Well," Marie let's out a huff, "I suppose I can't blame her for wanting to keep the town safe. You have to tell her to stop, though. It's...rude. And we're not interested in any trouble. We're private people is all."

Charlie holds up her hands. "We're on it. I promise."

I shift sideways, taking in the assortment of artwork.

Watercolors.

Landscapes.

I waggle my finger at the canvases. "Have you been to all these places?"

"Oh, yes." Marie's exuberance returns, the conversation about mom obviously smothered by my interest in the paintings. "I like lighthouses. My boyfriend says they're ugly, but I feel at home near them."

Gayle, I'm assuming. "Who doesn't? They're so rich in history."

"Exactly!" She shoots me a grin. "Michigan has terrific ones."

I store that in my memory bank. "I've never been, but with the Great Lakes, I'd imagine you could spend days discovering different lighthouses."

She points at a painting of a white one at the end of a long pier. "This is in St. Joseph. I lived there for a summer. It's my absolute favorite."

"What does your boyfriend do while you're visiting and painting them?" Charlie asks.

She looks over her collection with nostalgia. "Sometimes he comes with me."

So far, we've seen New York and Michigan so I peruse the others, noting landmarks I recognize. I'm hardly well-traveled but it's hard to miss St. Louis's Gateway Arch and the Liberty Bell in Philadelphia. Has Gayle been to these places with her, I wonder?

Charlie breaks away and inspects a folding table with neatly stacked brochures. She holds one up. "Can I take this?"

"Of course. My website is listed on there."

Excellent. I join Charlie and peer at the tri-fold brochure. "Is your entire inventory listed on it?"

Marie nods. "Yes. I've included a brief description of each location as well."

Oh, thank you. I love when people make things easy. Now we'll be able to note the places Marie—and possibly Gayle—have visited. More than likely we won't have timeframes, but we're only at the first step. We'll make a list and see where it leads.

We offer our goodbyes and dive into the crowd again, remaining silent until out of earshot of our target.

We reach the end of the block and take up residence beside a fire hydrant while we text Jerome, JJ, and Mom with our location.

I tuck my phone in my pocket and get back to business. "What do you think?"

Charlie's eyes gleam with that predatory hunger that overtakes her when working a case. "I think we're going to research any unsolved murders in those places. If we get any matches, I'm calling in every favor I'm owed and maybe we'll get some intel."

5

Charlie

*A*t three, I'm at the coffee shop a few blocks from the office, waiting for Alfonzo Baez.

The air-conditioning is better than ours, so I'm glad I offered to meet him here. Bonus, I can grab something to eat.

I have a tall iced coffee and a chicken avocado sandwich in front of me. Mom wanted to discuss the art festival, and I mostly wanted a shower and a few minutes of quiet time to think about Gayle and the bodies found in Virginia. Meg, thank goodness, talked Mom into going out for lunch, and I begged off, claiming a headache. This case is a giant one.

Marie appears like a normal artsy person, similar to Meg. There was nothing suspicious about her lighthouses, or behavior. Fortunately or not, Gayle was nowhere to be seen.

I'm still pissed he threatened Mom, but I almost can't blame him. It's bad enough your neighbor spies on you constantly, but then to return from vacation and find she was only down the lane from you?

Meg plans to look up Marie's website and dig into her background. After my meeting, I'll cross-check to see if it's possible Marie and Gayle's visits coincide with any cold cases or unsolved murders in those areas. It's a long shot, but if I find nothing, I can put this to rest. It probably won't be that easy because Mom will try to keep things stirred up, but if there's no link, she'll have to let it go.

Alfonzo Baez is medium-sized, with dark hair sprinkled with silvery strands and a mustache. He's wearing a black motorcycle jacket over a T-shirt, jeans, and boots. There's a bandana around his forehead, and his sunglasses are wired and reflective.

Not at all what I expected, but I can recognize the former agent in him from the swagger. He scans the handful of patrons, his attention swinging to me, as if I too have a sign over my head flashing "FBI."

He pulls out the empty chair at the two-person table, offering his hand. "You must be Helen Schock's daughter. I see the resemblance."

Interesting. Most think Meg favors her, but there's a touch around my eyes and chin that comes from her DNA. I shake his proffered hand. "Thank you for meeting me here. I'm sorry if I interrupted your plans." I point at his attire.

He sits and waves it off. "Heading out for a day trip. No problem at all."

I intend to keep this as brief as possible, so I get right to the point. "Mom claims you and your private cold case group are helping her look into our neighbor and some of his activities." I emphasize the last word, reluctant to call him a killer. "This has been an obsession of hers since Meg and I were children, and while all she has is a whole lot of circumstantial evidence, she's officially hired my sister and I to look into the man's comings and goings. I'm hoping to close this by giving her definitive proof he's innocent. Yesterday, she mentioned you'd connected a trip she took with my father, where Mr. Morton was also vacationing. Three bodies turned up in the nearby woods some years later. I was hoping you could give me more details."

"Your mother is a relentless investigator," Baez says. He tosses his sunglasses on the table, and wipes a bead of sweat from his forehead. "She's keeping me on my toes. I've been slowly working my way through our combined case notes, and there are several weekends when the neighbor was traveling that correspond to unsolved murders in that area. And yes, he was at Whitetop Mountain where three female bodies were discovered in 2004."

He doesn't realize this is my nightmare, the thing that took up my mother's time more than I did growing up. "We need something a lot stronger than that to consider it even circumstantial."

As a former profiler, I can read little ticks in people's expressions. He smiles, granting this is true. "Agreed," he says. "But it's a curious coincidence that in the summer of 1995, he was gone from Friday to Sunday multiple weekends, and at least one was the same timeframe your parents stayed in a similar fishing cabin up the road. The place was a rental for twenty years and changed hands several times. I'm still tracking down the owner from back then to see if he can confirm Mr. Morton rented it on either of the other weekends your mom noted he was gone."

This makes my ears perk up, and other parts of me sink. "How long were you with the Bureau? I don't believe we ever met, did we?"

"Before your time. I was a field agent for seven years before moving up. Twenty total, and I don't miss a day of it."

We share a chuckle, and part of me thinks he actually does miss it some days. I do, too. "Is there anything else you've come across that points to even the slimmest thread connecting Gayle with those murders, or any others?"

He fiddles with his sunglasses. "Like I mentioned, I'm working my way through the notes, but Helen's got a nose for crime. My concern is she might get herself in trouble. He could be dangerous, so I'm sticking close to her to keep her safe. If she hired you, along with working with us in the CSCC, she's serious about this."

"When I say she's been obsessed with this guy, I'm not kidding. Honestly, I'm surprised he hasn't taken out a restraining order."

"I've warned her to be careful. Investigating cold case murders could alert the killer and he, Morton or whoever it is, could come after her. Protecting her and the other members of my group is my number one priority."

"Ditto, believe me. I appreciate you looking out for her. Meg and I try. So does Dad, but Mom has a mind of her own. She doesn't alert us when she's walking into the lion's den."

He grins. "Because she knows you'll try and stop her."

"Precisely."

"I'd like to continue working the case, if you'll have me," Baez says. Yep, he misses the work. "Pro-bono, of course. Between the two of us, we can comb through everything, hash things out. It will give you extra creditability with your mother, if there isn't anything there. I've got no skin in the game, so think of me as an outside, independent resource."

It's a good idea, and he's right. I could show Mom all the evidence in the world that Gayle is innocent, and she wouldn't believe me. An independent source like Alfonzo, with the same FBI background I have, and many years of experience, might do the trick.

I extend a hand over the table. "Sounds like a deal. I never turn down qualified help, especially when it's free."

He shakes it, and laughs. "She told me you were smart."

We exchange a few more general ideas about where to go next, and he leaves.

I'm finishing my sandwich and iced coffee when JJ texts me. *We still on for tonight?*

On our way home from the festival, he mentioned bringing over a movie. I told him to throw in a gallon of ice cream, and I'd consider it a date.

A second text follows. *I have three flavors.*

He knows me well, or maybe I'm simply too easy.

You're on, I reply.

6

Meg

Marie's website wasn't bad. It wasn't good either, but I'm not exactly an expert, so what do I know?

After Charlie begged off, Jerome and I spent another hour with my mom, then had her drop us off at the train station.

I now sit in my home, one half of the duplex I share with my sister, putting my laptop to work. Jerome is beside me on the sofa and the faded scent of his spicy soap distracts me, launching my thoughts to waking up in bed with my guy.

I love him. I know I do. He brings a level of calm and understanding that's long been missing in my life. For that, I'll always be grateful.

He peers at the screen as I scroll through the featured paintings.

"What are we looking for?" He asks.

As if I should know? Welcome to the land of Schock where

we're not altogether sure what we're doing until we stumble upon information that could, in fact, blow a case wide open.

"Charlie met with one of the guys from that cold case group mom hooked up with. Turns out, he thinks she's on to something."

"Seriously?"

I pause briefly at a navy blue lighthouse then click to the next photo. "Scary, I know. Apparently, this guy is a former FBI agent—which immediately gives him credibility with Charlie. He's retired now and has a handle on my mom's research."

Click.

Click.

A bright red lighthouse fills my screen and I zoom in on it. It's cute and resides in the great state of New York along the Hudson River. The little red lighthouse from my childhood. The same painting we saw at the festival.

I click to the next. "Gayle took trips to Virginia during the summer of '95 and the Fed says three bodies were discovered in the area where he stayed."

"Okay. How is this relevant to you digging around her website?"

I hold up the page of notes I took when Charlie relayed her conversation with Alfonzo. "Marie told us she paints places she's visited. Charlie wants me to see if the Virginia cabin where Gayle stayed comes up in any of them."

"You think it'll be that easy?"

He has a point. "Probably not, but we need to start somewhere."

I click through a series of paintings. Lighthouse after lighthouse after lighthouse, each with its own charm, but for the love of God, how many could someone paint?

For the next thirty minutes, I call out the names of them along with the dates listed in their description. Jerome uses his phone to do internet searches, rattling off locations and basic facts. By the end of the session we have a list of thirteen states.

And Virginia is most definitely one of them.

"The dates don't match," I say. "Not even close."

According to Marie's brief write up under the Virginia paintings, she visited those particular lighthouses in 2007, 2010, and 2014.

"Are you really surprised by that?"

I treat it as a rhetorical question and don't bother answering. Serial killers, I've learned, are often brilliant. Anyone who would allow their girlfriend to publicly post dates and locations of their kills deserves to be imprisoned just for being stupid.

Therefore, I surmise, this is probably a useless endeavor.

I set my laptop aside and rest my head back while Jerome studies the notes we've made.

"How long has this guy lived across the street?"

"He moved here in the early nineties. At first, it was idle curiosity because he really only went out at night. The more free time my mother had, the worse it got. When we were in school? Forget it. She sat in that window all day. It was maddening. My friends thought she was crazy."

A small smile plays on Jerome's soft lips. Gosh, he's cute. I battle my urge to touch him. To run my fingers over his solid jaw and supple mouth. One day, I will sculpt him.

"I'm no detective," he says, "but couldn't Charlie look at when Gayle first moved in? He probably has a mortgage. Those require loan applications. Maybe what he did for a living back then might tell us something."

It's a good thought, but Mom was way ahead of him so I slowly shake my head. "Tried that. The house is a rental."

"Come on. It's been twenty years."

"It has, indeed. An older couple lived there when we were kids. The husband died and the wife soon after. The remaining family members were fighting over the will and wound up renting to Gayle while they sorted it all out. Once the estate was settled, one of those home rental companies bought it. Since Gayle had been living there and paying rent regularly, they only required him to sign a new lease and leave an extra month's deposit in case he skipped."

Jerome's bottom lip rolls out. "Wow. Gotta say, she's good if she got all that on him."

His appreciation of her analytical skills ignites a burst of pride. "She loves research. It made her an excellent reporter. I think that's where Charlie gets her investigative skills."

Jerome ponders this for a moment then shrugs. "Still, it's a long time to be a renter."

"Which only fuels my mother's suspicion. It's easier to hide an identity when there are no credit apps involved."

"Maybe he's not a serial killer."

"Ya think?"

I laugh, but Jerome's narrowed stare tells me he doesn't share my humor.

"I'm not kidding," he says. "Why can't he be in witness protection or something? Back in the nineties, the mob was huge in New York and you just found some New York lighthouses. Maybe he's a rat."

Who knew my artsy Jerome even understood street slang? It reminds me how much I've yet to learn and fills me with excitement.

Each day lately is like unwrapping a new gift.

Gifts aside, Jerome has a point. For years, my mother's working theory has been that Gayle is a murderer.

What if he is and testified against a bunch of other murderers?

Jerome sets the notes on the sofa cushion and folds his hands in his lap. When he closes his eyes, I take in the lush thickness of his dark eyelashes. I like to tease him about them, insisting on butterfly kisses every time we say goodnight.

It's become routine. Some women want the euphoric rush new relationships bring, the absolute high of being in love.

Me? I have enough drama in my life. I want the reverse. I want boring, steady comfort.

Jerome's eyes snap open and he busts me staring at him. "You're thinking," he says. "What about?"

"Butterfly kisses and rats."

He waggles his eyebrows at me. "You like that theory, huh?"

"It's a good one. Someone living in witness protection would lay low, right? Maybe not go out when most folks are doing errands and whatnot. If he sticks to evening, darkness keeps him shadowed."

"I agree."

I reach for my laptop and hit the spacebar, bringing it to life again. "He might not be in witness protection. But if he's on the run, he'd probably behave in the same manner. Staying out of sight and such."

Jerome tilts his head, watching me as I click on my browser. "What are you doing?"

"A search for the FBI's most wanted lists from the early nineties, the years before Gayle moved in across the street."

7

Charlie

*I*t's a good day to be Charlie Schock.

I sit in my air-conditioned office, rocking in my chair and staring at a framed photograph I've hung on the wall. It's a painting of mountains, woods, and vast open blue sky that reminds me of my favorite U.S. District Attorney's eyes.

JJ bought it at the fair for me, and I have to admit, it catches my attention throughout the day and makes me pause to take a deep breath. I can almost picture myself there, the clean mountain air, a backpack, and JJ. We've discussed our bucket lists. Hiking with him is on mine.

In front of me is a stack of seven cases. The rush in my blood and the tick of my pulse is like that of a sprinter at the starting line, waiting for the gun to go off. There are too many jobs, too much work, but I'm excited anyway. I can't wait to dig in.

The stress of being successful is one I thrive on, as does

Matt who is currently down the hall, on the phone for the case I've assigned him. Like me, he welcomes the workload. We could still use another hand, and if this uptick in cases continues and brings in the dollars to pay for it, the temporary position could turn permanent.

Out front, Haley sings along with her playlist. Meg is MIA, and that's okay. My sister has finally gotten a life, and she doesn't haunt the office as much as she used to. The missing and the unidentified do not trouble her obsessively now, thanks to Jerome, and for that, I'm thankful. She's working normal hours, taking long lunches, and sometimes not coming in until well after the day is in full-swing.

Haley stops singing and I hear the arrival of a visitor. I turn my attention to the first case, but the familiar voice of Alfonzo makes me pause. He texted earlier to let me know he had a condensed file on the three bodies found in Virginia that might be linked to Mom's case against Gayle.

Haley shows him to my office. The biker is gone, and today, he's dressed in a white button-down, charcoal gray jacket, and black jeans.

He's still wearing motorcycle boots, so I guess his inner rebel is alive and well. He's shaved and has combed back his salt and pepper strands, and looks nice—more like the agent he used to be, and probably still is at heart.

He smiles and we shake over the desk. He plops a large white envelope on top of my blotter. "Here you go. I condensed the details about the bodies, the identities of the two we have, and their family members' information. If you want to comb through the originals, I'm sure I can get copies."

I motion him into one of the chairs and resume my seat, opening the envelope and glancing through the neat set of notes. If I didn't already know he was former FBI, I might guess it from the way he's categorized everything and cross-referenced certain details, in color, no less. "I appreciate this. Saves me a ton of time."

"Happy to help." He glances around, his eyes admiring the functional furniture, sparse decoration, and landing for a moment on the painting. "No point in you having to hunt through all of those yourself when I've done the work. I'm sure you have better things to do."

He motions at the stack of folders next to my right arm. "Business is good, huh?"

"I don't like publicity, but in recent months we've had a lot and the exposure has been advantageous. "It's so good in fact,"—I lean back and steeple my fingers—"I'm looking to hire part-time help. You don't happen to know anyone who might be available?"

Dad taught me that you never know what you're going to get when you throw your line out, but testing the waters can't hurt.

The grin Al shoots me tells me he knows exactly what— who—I'm fishing for. "I might know a guy. What kind of work does it involve?"

Mom totally respects this guy, and my own casual background check confirmed he's thought of quite highly by his former Bureau coworkers. I'm hoping to track down his partner, the real litmus test to reveal any quirks or oddities that'll upset our group. Meg, Matt, and I are a team. Our system is tried and true, and not everyone will add to that. "The usual— surveillance, a lot of paperwork, bad coffee."

"I still have my investigator's license, and I'm a sucker for bad coffee." He glances around again, as if this somehow gives him a feel for the job opportunity I've extended. "I suppose the pay stinks as well?"

I nod, enjoying banter with someone who's been in the field. "You know it. Small time operations like ours can't afford big salaries, but we offer perks."

One of his bushy eyebrows rises. "Health insurance? Paid vacation?"

I look at him as if he's daft. "Whoa, let's not go crazy. We do happen to have seasonal tickets to the Wizards' games. Each employee gets to pick at least three sets for the season."

Little does he know neither Meg nor I care about basketball. I happen to have a client that's on the team's office staff and likes to pay his occasional bill this way. Matt and Haley both enjoy them, so it all works out.

Al rubs his chin as if considering this as a real perk. "Any chance to get a company car or at least a new cell out of the gig?"

I throw my head back and laugh. "You dream big, don't you? We reimburse mileage, and if you have to make calls that put you over your monthly limit, I'm sure we can make an adjustment in your paycheck."

He nods like this is a decent negotiation. "Case-by-case basis to start? I get to pick them, of course."

This would actually be perfect, except for the part that he gets the intriguing and easy investigations and leaves the less-than-desirable ones. "We'll work something out."

I hear the buzzer on the front door open again, and wonder who our new visitor is. Clients make appointments, drop-ins are rare.

"Can I have twenty-four hours to think about it?" Alfonzo asks.

He's stalling. Maybe trying to make me believe he doesn't miss his Bureau days. "Of course." I set my hand on top of the folders. "These babies aren't going anywhere overnight. There are a couple of pretty good ones, too. A former FBI agent could kick them out in no time."

Dangling the carrot. He nods slowly, still acting as though he's contemplating the job. "What might seal the deal is getting a bonus for those I close fast."

"You're a tough negotiator."

He gives me a broad, knowing smile. "Why do you think I retired early?"

In the distance, I hear JJ, asking if I'm in. Haley tells him I have a visitor, but of course, this doesn't stop him from barging down the hallway and appearing in my doorway. He glances at Alfonzo, then at me, then back to my guest. "Hey. Hope I'm not interrupting."

He knows he is, but doesn't care by the look on his face. "Al brought information that might help us solve Mom's case," I say.

Alfonzo stands to face him, holding out a hand. "Alfonzo Baez. You must be JJ Carrington."

JJ hesitates a brief second before shaking it. "I don't believe we've met."

I shoot JJ a questioning glance. I'd already told him about Alfonzo and the connection he made to the cabin where Gayle stayed in Virginia all those years ago. Still, I come around my desk and make official introductions. Once that's completed, I ask JJ, "Was there something important you needed?"

The set of his shoulders and the thrust of his chest as he puts his hands on his hips, brushing back his jacket, tells me there's a little alpha male rising to the surface. JJ exudes it all the time, but this is another level, and it makes me peek at Al, seeing him in a different light.

Surely, JJ doesn't think...

"I have business to discuss with you," he says to me. "I was hoping we could grab an early lunch. I'll be in meetings the rest of the day."

"I'll be right back," I tell Al, before grabbing JJ's arm and leading him out and toward the reception area.

"Business?" I ask under my breath.

He gives me a look that suggests there's something he wants

to tell me, but a glance at Haley, then toward my office, has him pushing it aside. "Can you do lunch or not?"

It's barely eleven. "Even with your help over the weekend, I'm behind on two pressing cases. Is it critical? Could we discuss it tonight over dinner?"

He clamps his jaw shut, starts to say something, then clamps it shut again. He glances at his watch. "I'll probably be busy until five or six. I'll swing by after that if I can."

There's definitely something he wants to discuss, but not in front of Haley. "We can use Meg's office," I suggest, too curious to let this go, "if that would help."

Silent communication flows between us, and I know he's considering it. Then he shakes his head. "It can wait until tonight. Sorry for barging in."

He leans forward and brushes a kiss on my forehead before turning and walking out.

Haley stares after him, her eyes dreamy. "You are so lucky, Charlie."

"Wipe the drool from your mouth." I start back down the hallway and Alfonzo pops out of my office. I smile at him. "Apologies for that."

He motions toward the front. "Everything okay?"

Maybe. "Fine. Would you like some coffee? We can continue our meeting."

I hear a ring and the back door opens, Meg and Jerome filing in. "Sorry, I'm late," Meg calls out.

Once again, I make introductions. I motion for Al to return to my office, but he shakes his head. "I have to skedaddle. Nice to meet you, Meg, Jerome." He nods at each of them. "Let me know if you have questions about the file," he tells me. "Or if there's more I can do to help."

He smiles and leaves us standing in the hallway.

"Don't forget about the job offer," I call after him.

He waves over his shoulder, says good-bye to Haley, and walks out. I like that he's nice to our receptionist.

Meg and Jerome follow me into my office. "That's Alfonzo?" Meg asks, dropping her purse on the floor and commandeering the chair Al just left. Jerome takes the other.

"He brought information about the three women found in Virginia." I flick a glance at Jerome, then back to Meg. Jerome is not part of our team, nor is he law enforcement or a private detective. The agent in me resists sharing details with him about crimes or the investigations we have going on.

"If you have time, Meg,"—I make it a point to emphasis her name and leave Jerome out—"maybe you could read through this and see if there's anything we should follow up on."

"Sure, we can work on that." She leans forward, shuffling through her purse, and pulls out a crumpled piece of paper. "Jerome and I had this idea, after searching for the lighthouse locations. Well, it was kind of his idea."

I flinch internally. Apparently, he's part of this whether I want him to be or not.

Meg goes on. "We got to talking about how it's possible Gayle isn't a serial killer, but maybe he's still on the lam for something. I searched the FBI's most wanted lists between 1991 and 1999 and we came up with this."

Meg hands me the paper and I scan the list of names. "Okay...?" I'm not sure what I'm supposed to conclude from this. "You think one of these people could be Gayle?"

"I scanned the photos of those I could find," Meg says. "Without age progression, I can't be positive, but none look like him to me. Maybe he was tied in with one of them."

"He could be in witness protection," Jerome offers. "What if he was going to testify against one of those guys? Or maybe he did, and the Feds put him in the protection program. He's been living off taxpayer dollars for all these years right across the street from you guys!"

I try not to show my lack of appreciation for his imagination. "A possibility."

"We don't have much else." Meg's face tells me she's scared I won't humor Jerome. "I found nothing with the lighthouses. At least this is a starting point."

"You want to research each of these people to see if you can find a connection to Gayle, who could be living under a false name if he's in WITSEC." I inwardly cringe at the time that type of investigation might take, and odds are low they'll find anything. Yet, both Meg and Jerome look at me with hope in their eyes. "What about the hundreds of cases the FBI closed around that time that he might have testified in? Again, if he's a criminal and a snitch, Gayle Morton isn't his real name. I'm not sure where you should begin."

They both nod, still excited about this avenue, and now filled with determination.

"Don't you have contacts in the WITSEC program who could point us in the right direction?" Meg asks.

"That's U.S. Marshal territory, and they aren't going to share that kind of information with a former agent."

She sighs.

I hate to dash any hopes, but we're already incredibly understaffed. "Plus, it's going to take an enormous amount of man hours, Meg."

She gestures over her shoulder toward the front of the office. "You just offered that guy a job, right? Why can't he look into some of this with us? Save us a lot of time. He's former FBI, like you. I assume he's some sort of expert on criminals, and the witness protection program...and stuff."

Yes, a bunch of stuff is what I feel we have at the moment with Mom's case. It's similar to cotton candy, sticky and sweet, but there's nothing to it.

Eyeing the files on my desk, my mind is already wandering to getting some real work done today, and not just

MISTY EVANS & ADRIENNE GIORDANO

chasing leads that'll probably go nowhere and waste a lot of time.

Bright side? Jerome will work for free, thanks to my sister.

The cases Al gave us are old, and although the killer was never brought to justice, two of the three bodies were identified and the families notified. The information is public record, nothing top secret, and no one's looked at these cases in years, outside of Al.

What can it hurt to put Jerome to work, and let Meg jump in with both feet, as well? She currently doesn't have any skulls to reconstruct, and she has a nose for tracking criminals. They can work together to check into the murdered women, and the list.

"Okay." I sound like a broken record. "If you two want to look into them, go for it. Meg, mark off the cases that were closed and examine the testimonies against the defendants because that will be public record. Anything trips your radar; make a note and I'll have Al—if he comes to work for us— review the details. Jerome, you take the open cases. Again, if anything seems like it could lead to Gayle, we can ask Matt to contact Taylor and see if she'll share details."

Jerome jumps up and claps. "Awesome."

Meg eyes me, slightly skeptical. "You think this could be legit? That Gayle's not a killer, but maybe another type of criminal?"

I've seen some incredibly improbable circumstances and situations in my line of work. I rarely discount anything. "I'll follow the serial killer angle and start contacting family members of the deceased women. You two work on this other angle."

Meg looks delighted, and Jerome is happy because she is.

My sister stands and starts listing things they're going to do. They head to the conference room, and I glance over Alfonzo's notes.

46

I appreciate how they're laid out, identifying similarities between the three young women, the cause of death, the consistencies between the shallow graves they were buried in and the time frame all three died.

Al wasn't a profiler, but I can see the language in his notes. I read through those in more detail, developing my own portrait of the killer.

From the forensic autopsies, all three women were in their late twenties. The two identified victims were brunettes, curvy, single. They hailed from rough backgrounds—single mothers, absentee fathers, troublemakers in school, and as adults, had difficulty holding jobs. One was described by a family member as a "slut." No interview notes from the other victim's family.

All of them died from asphyxiation and were buried wrapped in garbage bags, landing in shallow graves. No signs they were killed in the woods, only disposed of there. The original investigation cited that the deaths most likely occurred within a few years of each other.

Hard to tell if they were premeditated. Strangulation is usually a sign of rage, so probably not. The killer obviously thought out where to hide them, however, and he or she had a familiarity with the woods in order to turn it into a burial ground.

As I continue to take notes, I pause and think about the dozen serials I profiled while at the Bureau, and the ones we caught and brought to trial. As a forensic psychologist, I examined and testified in court on the competence and mental state of at least six. Several used strangulation—either with their hands or a garrote.

From what I know about Gayle, the profile in my head of a classic serial killer with a fixation or obsession for strangulation doesn't match him at all.

8

Meg

Jerome drops into the chair across from me, his hazel eyes twinkling under the conference room's florescent overhead light. Who knew my artist boyfriend would enjoy research so much?

I smile as I hand him a folder. "You're having fun."

"Anything I do with you is fun." For added effect, he waggles his eyebrows. A move that doesn't just nudge my hormones, but sends them into a ravenous roar.

Even thinking about Jerome—and sex with him—gets me warm and gooey inside.

Me.

The girl who talks to dead people.

Go figure.

Except, this is business that includes my mother. That alone is enough to douse my lust. Throw in Mom's obsession with her neighbor and I might as well be a nun. I can feel my eggs drying up already.

"Let's get to work," I say.

Work now, canoodling later.

Jerome rolls his eyes. "I take back what I said about you being fun."

"There's time later for that. Now, I need to help my mother." I point at the folder I've just handed him. "That's the first batch. We'll each take half."

"What are we doing with them?"

"Research. Whatever you can find. I'd start with determining where they are now. If they've been caught and are incarcerated, see where."

He flips the folder open and peruses the first page. "What will that tell us?"

"I'm not sure yet. We'll figure out who's still at-large and who isn't. Then we'll see if any are from Virginia. We know Gayle was in Virginia on three separate weekends in 1995."

"A lot of people visit there."

"Within fourteen miles of a burial site? Three women, all strangled and wrapped in garbage bags?" I shake my head. "Sorry, handsome. That's not flying."

Jerome lets out a low whistle. "I see your point."

"Exactly."

He looks down at the open folder again. "So I'm looking for any Virginia connection."

"Yes."

I watch him for a few seconds, taking in his long eyelashes and straight nose. The way his shaggy hair curls around his cheeks.

I love him.

Probably always have.

It's terrifying and yet it's as if sunlight on a winter day has burst through a cloud inside me. I've always known I felt...

something. Even admitted to myself it was love, just not the I-will-take-a-bullet kind that has eluded me for so long.

Now?

No denying it. Not to myself anyway. Whether I'm willing to let Jerome in on that secret is another matter. Our connection is deep. I've even used the L word with him before, but not in this context. We've skirted around it by saying how much we care and that we'd be miserable without the other, yada, yada.

Hell, I could say that about my sister or Matt. I love them both also.

So, Jerome? Yes, he knows. He just doesn't understand the extent of it.

"You're staring," he says, his gaze still locked on his folder.

I am indeed. "Sorry."

No, I'm not.

I give up on thoughts of love and Jerome's eyelashes and dig into my own folder.

An hour later, we've barely said two words and my ambition for this project is starting to wane. Plus, I have a fatigue headache brewing behind my right eye. Soon, I'll need a quick ten-minute mediation to give my mind and body time to recharge.

But I'm making progress. I've researched five of my eight fugitives. Four are locked up and one, a money launderer, is probably living on his ill-gotten gains and exploring the South Pacific in a sixty-foot sailboat.

I flip the page and say hello to one Christopher "Sven" Svenson, a thirty-two-year-old bank robber wanted in four states. New York, New Jersey, Connecticut and Missouri.

Odd. Three of the four are in the tri-state area. Missouri stands out. I read on to find Sven was born and bred there and chose to kick off his thieving ways in the bank three miles from his parents' home.

Lovely.

I study his wanted poster, noting his height, weight, any cautionary notes. At the time, the FBI considered him armed and dangerous and traveling with his longtime girlfriend, a woman named Evelyn Jacoby. I jot that down for further research, but first tap Sven's name into my phone.

A list of links pops up, the FBI most wanted being the first. I bypass that and scroll through news reports on his robberies. Fifteen banks over a six-month period.

Busy guy.

The next stops me—dammit.

Sven hadn't just been captured; he'd been killed. Late 1999. A tipster revealed his location and the subsequent FBI raid left him and his bank-robbing buddies thoroughly devastated by gunfire and...well...dead.

"That's disappointing," I mutter.

"What?"

I lift my head, my gaze meeting Jerome's. "Hitting steel walls here. Four of my guys are in prison and one is dead. I'm chasing my tail."

Jerome shrugs. "It's research. That's what happens. Keep going. You never know."

I roll my eyes. Thank you, Confucius.

I mean, could he not come up with something a tad more motivating?

This isn't his fault though. I close my eyes, draw a breath of stale air then slowly release it. I hate being locked in a closed-off room. Eventually, the energy becomes too heavy. Too...stuck.

"I'm not being a jerk, Meg."

My guy. He knows me so well. "I know. It's just—"

"Frustrating."

"Yes. Have you found anything? Please, give me some good news."

Slowly, he shakes his head. Back and forth, back and forth, each movement like a stab to my already aching head.

"Sorry, sweets. I've got zip. Not done yet, though."

Terrific.

Rallying myself for the last few reports, I give a firm nod. "Let's finish this and meditate. Then we'll get out of here. Get some fresh air."

"I like it," Jerome says.

Like me, he's a fan of meditation. As creatives, we have a keen understanding of how mindfulness fuels artistic expression.

A soft knock sounds and Charlie pops her head in. As usual, she's all pulled together. Perfect hair, perfect lipstick, perfect clothing while I'm...wilting.

"Hi. Sorry to interrupt."

Actually, I'm thankful for the distraction. "No prob. What's up?"

"Mom is here. She wants an update."

Of course she does.

For years this case has driven our mother to near-madness. Now she's become our client, turning over her research, which, knowing her, was probably more difficult than childbirth.

As much as I'd like to share any potential leads, we have nothing solid.

I shake my head. "We don't have anything yet. It's a bust so far."

"Are you done?"

"No. We both have a few more to look at."

Charlie purses her lips and gives me her squinty eyes. "We need to stall Mom. You have research to be done."

My sister. Brilliant. "You want to give Mom the rest."

"It'll keep her occupied and buy us time."

I meet Jerome's eye just as he flips his folder closed. "Works for me."

Pushing out of my chair, I straighten my reports. "Ditto that. We'll let Mom chase her tail instead of us."

9

Charlie

Six o'clock comes and I haven't heard from JJ, no doubt because of the meetings. I take a bath, put on a silky robe, and bring his favorite strappy stilettos to the dining room with me. I'll slip them on as soon as he texts me to let me know he's coming.

I picked up a rotisserie chicken on the way home and some sides. I open a cab sav and pour a glass, sit in front of my laptop, and start working.

One of my clients calls an hour later, telling me her husband is working late again, and she wants me to get the pictures she needs to prove he's having an affair. I don't usually do cheating spouse cases—Matt does. But in this situation? The husband is an esteemed member of our city council, and the divorce proceedings will have to be handled carefully if she goes through with them, since he has deep pockets and a bunch of people around the city, including two judges, in them.

The last thing I feel like doing on this hot summer night is trekking out to follow him and sit for hours in my car, hoping to get a picture of him with his girlfriend. I text Matt, who's home alone—he was bemoaning the fact Taylor was going out with friends before he left the office—and he's more than happy to do the surveillance. I send him the details and go back to the research I'm doing for another client.

When my doorbell rings a few minutes later, I scramble from the table to grab the stilettos. JJ didn't text me, and I fumble with one of them, the strap not cooperating with my fingers in my haste to switch from private investigator to sex kitten. The new lipstick I bought—a man-eating red—is waiting on the table by the door.

It's unusual for him to not simply let himself in. He has a key. The thought pulls me up short, and I wobble to the door, one shoe on and one off, to peer out the transom window.

From the other side, my mother calls, "Charlie, it's me!"

For half a second, I bow my head. I thought we gave Mom plenty to keep her busy for another day or so. Why is she here?

Begrudgingly, I open the door. She brushes past, eyes flicking over my robe and the shoe disparity, but not seeming to register that I've decided to relax this evening.

I need more wine.

She carries a binder and what looks like an old telephone book in her arms, making her way into the dining room and slamming the two on the table.

"Mom?" I close the door and follow. "What's up?"

She looks at me as though I'm dense. "I'm here to work on Gayle's case."

I pointedly glance at my stuff on the table. "I have other things to do tonight."

She scans the robe, the shoe I'm holding, and glances at my laptop. "Fine, but I need some help. I'd like you to look up a couple of the hardware stores in the area where those bodies were found. I need to know if they're still in business, and their phone number."

"Why?"

"The bodies were found in contractor grade garbage bags. Those had to come from somewhere. Gayle might've gotten them from a hardware store nearby, and maybe I can figure out which one and call around..."

Even to her own ears this must sound a little farfetched, because she trails off and looks at the phone book. "I'm sure I can trace Gayle buying the supplies he needed to bury them."

The phone book is from the county the cabin is in. It looks to be a good ten or fifteen years old. "Where did you find that?" I point.

"I have all of them from our local area and some from the bordering states, going back years." She lays a hand on the top of it. "These are history, Charlie. My news days taught me that. You never know when you might need the information they provide about the past."

"There's this thing called the internet," I say gently, teasing. "You'd be surprised how much information is out there."

She huffs. "That's exactly why I'm here, Miss Smarty Pants. There are six hardware stores listed in the Yellow Pages, but most don't have the same number anymore. The two I was able to connect with don't have records that old, at least that's what they told me. But if Gayle used a check or credit card..."

"If he's a criminal and has been able to outfox law enforcement all these years, I doubt he was careless enough to use any type of traceable payment."

Mom makes her way into the kitchen to pour a glass of the wine. "I have to follow all leads, no matter how insignificant they may seem. It's our credo at the CSCC. It always served me when I was at the paper, too."

It's not a bad tenet. Seemingly insignificant leads have

provided turning points in many cases. "What about the criminals on the most wanted list? Did you finish with those?"

She leans against the counter. "That was a dead end. A total waste of my time. Al and I blew through them in an hour."

Thank you, Al. *Not.*

She takes a deep gulp of wine, scans the label on the bottle. "All I need is for you to dig up these other hardware stores and their numbers. They probably simply have new ones. It's a lead, Charlie. I'm following it."

I force myself to take a deep breath as I unbuckle the single stiletto still on my foot. I can't deny her investigative nose, and I have the feeling she needs one of Meg's pot brownies. Or more of my wine. Either way, it won't hurt to humor her. "Okay. It won't take but a minute."

It suddenly dawns on her that I might have company and she pushes off the counter, looking toward the living room and beyond to my bedroom.

"Is JJ here?" She doesn't wait for me to respond, going to the hallway and calling into the rest of the house, "JJ! It's me, Helen. Charlie and I are working on the case. Why don't you come help us?"

I take a seat. "He's not here, Mom."

She returns to the table and sits as well. "Do you always run around your house in the evening in a fancy robe and hooker shoes?"

I glance at her over the laptop. She grins.

"Maybe that's what I like to do. It helps me relax."

She pulls the phone book from her stack and mumbles under her breath. "And they think *I'm* crazy."

"Not crazy, just driven, and we understand that. Meg and I are, too. But, Mom, all you had to do was call. You didn't have to drive clear across town to ask me."

"Your dad is gone. I had nothing better to do." She flips

open the book where she has it marked. "Besides, we can get more done if I'm here."

And there's the real reason she's here...no one is home to talk to about the case. Who knows where Al is. She slides the book to me and I see where she's circled various ads from that time period.

"JJ is coming over soon," I tell her. "We'll do a quick search, but even if these hardware stores are still in existence, and have a number listed, it's eight-thirty, Mom. They're not open."

She ignores me, dragging the binder over and flipping through it. She searches in her purse and pulls out a pen. "I'm ready when you are."

I roll my eyes, call up a search engine, and plug in the first one. "Denny's Hardware Store. Closed in 1999."

We spend the next few minutes going through them. There's an Ace Hardware still in business and actually does have a different number. She looks like we've struck gold when I read it. She roots around in her bag, yanks out her cell and dials. Surprise, surprise, no one answers.

She hangs up, frustrated. "What time do they open? We should be there in person to question them."

The psychologist in me knows this obsession isn't healthy, and she could probably use anti-anxiety meds, but I remind myself she's not hurting anyone. I try to look at this as if it's simply a hobby. An intense one, but still harmless.

"I love you, Mom, but we are not driving to Virginia at the crack of dawn to harass a clerk first thing in the morning when the store opens. Tomorrow, you can call and ask politely if they have records from the 90s. You realize, even if they do, they won't turn that information over to you, most likely. There are legal channels we'll have to go through in order to get personal information about customers."

"Fine." She rises with a dramatic flourish and flips the phone book closed. She flips the binder shut as well, tosses the pen back in her purse. "Where is JJ? Is he the one that'll have to get the warrant for us in order to obtain it?"

Deep breath. "One step at a time," I coach. "Let's reconvene in the office at nine. Meg can be there with you when you call, and if there's any chance they still have records from the time period in question, we'll move forward, okay?"

My phone buzzes with a text. JJ's on his way. I stand. "I hate to rush you out, but I have work to do tonight."

Mom leans on the table, a shaky smile on her lips. "What cases? Maybe I could help?"

Oh, hell no. "A high-profile cheating spouse, an employee who's embezzling money from the company, a partner in a small business who's trying to blackmail the other partner."

She taps the binder. "You're the expert on serial killers, right? I think my case is a lot more important than any of those. I'd appreciate your support and cooperation helping me track down every lead I can. You might take a few pointers from Alfonzo. At least he understands the consequences of letting someone like Gayle run around free as a bird."

"Mom, you have a nose for this stuff. If it weren't for you, I may have never thought about being an FBI agent. I might not have ever been interested in crime in general." I move toward the front door. "But try to see things from my point of view. Even with all of the research you've done through the years, there's no physical proof Gayle is a serial killer. The only way a law enforcement officer can act on this is if we have evidence that shows he could be. Everything you have is completely circumstantial and can be explained away."

"Well, then,"—she puts the strap of her purse over her shoulder, looking grim—I'll leave you to your important cases. But you should let me help. Like you said, I have a nose for it."

She picks up her stack. "Maybe I'll visit your sister."

This is supposed to be a dig, but I have the feeling Meg won't be any more excited to see Mom than I was. The laughter

I've heard coming from her side suggests she and Jerome are having a good night.

I lay a hand on our mother's arm. "We're doing everything we can. I know it's frustrating, but we're following the clues. It takes time. One of the best leads for you to follow right now is figuring out the identity of the third woman. That's a giant mystery in all this. Ask Al where the remains are being kept. Let's see if we can get some info on her. If the two of you work on that, it would be extremely helpful."

Her eyes light up and the defensiveness eases. "What are you and Meg doing next?"

"Interviewing family members of the identified victims."

"I thought Alfonzo gave you the notes on the interviews the police did."

"I'd like to speak to a few of them in person. I have follow-up questions to see if any might know or remember someone fitting Gayle's description."

This new direction seems to excite her. She hugs her binder. "Oh. That's a good idea."

I gently guide her toward the door. "What we need is a picture of Gayle from that time period. Do you happen to have any?"

"Of course. I'll look for it tonight."

"Perfect." I open the door, the heat and humidity of the night rushing in. "Let's meet in the morning. You and Meg can call the hardware store while I look into contacting the family members. Bring the picture, and I'll scan it to send to anyone willing to talk to us."

"It's a plan." She practically skips down the front steps to the car. I stand in the door and wave as she pulls away.

Phew. Another bullet dodged.

When JJ arrives, I'm in the stilettos with the man-eating lipstick in place. I greet him before he can knock, and his tired face brightens as he takes in my appearance.

Dinner is laid out, and he shrugs off his suit jacket, downs half a glass of wine, and rolls up his shirt sleeves before he digs into the meal.

We don't talk much, and afterward, the robe comes off and the stilettos stay on. Once we retire to the bedroom, he finally tells me what he wanted to talk about earlier.

"You need to be careful with Baez," he says.

My head is resting on his chest as his fingers toy with my hair. "Why?"

"Eight months before retiring, he was under investigation by the attorney general."

I rise up on one elbow. "What? That can't be right. I already looked into his background." There's no way I'd offer anyone a job without doing that first. "I even talked to a few friends at the Bureau who were around when he was on the job. Nobody had anything but praise for him. With his close rate on high profile cases, he's a hero."

JJ's eyes settle on my face. "That was part of the issue. It was internal and hush-hush. There was suspicion that he was using entrapment methods, leading to these quick and easy close rates."

A lump of dread settles in my stomach. I can't believe this. I'm a profiler, a psychologist. My bullshit radar is extremely touchy—I can pick out bad apples a mile away. "He retired with commendations in his file that make the rest of us look like amateurs."

"It didn't go anywhere because there wasn't enough evidence. The Justice Department had a snitch—someone inside one of these criminal cases that Baez led who claimed to have information regarding the entrapment issues. The snitch didn't come through, and scuttlebutt claims Baez got to him first. It's one of the reasons your friend retired early."

I sit up all the way and shake my head. "Alfonzo was a dirty agent?"

JJ rubs his hands over his face and throws his arms above his head. He stares up at the ceiling. "There's no proof, but an awful lot of suspicion. That's enough for me." His gaze returns to lock on mine. "Be careful, Charlie."

It's hard for me to believe we're talking about the same guy. "Everything I've seen and heard about him is positive. Hell, he started this citizens group for closing cold cases."

JJ sits up now, facing me. He brushes back a strand of my hair, his fingers grazing my shoulder. "He may be a hero, who knows?" He takes my hand and kisses my knuckles one by one. "As always, you're free to do whatever you think is best, but please, for me, be careful."

There's a tickle under my ribs. A warning. I can't stand dirty agents. And if this one is misleading Mom and her group of do-gooders, I'll kick his ass.

Sighing heavily, I push JJ flat on the bed and curl up in his arms.

10

Meg

*J*ust before eight, my sister emerges from her side of our duplex as I'm saying goodbye to Jerome on my tiny patch of a front porch. The sun is shining, birds are chirping and by the look on Charlie's face, she's about to ruin my blissful moment.

"Morning," she says, giving us fair warning in case we decide on some PDA.

Jerome pecks me lightly on the lips, a simple gesture that screams of familiarity and...belonging. Commitment, if I dare say it.

I love it so much it's almost painful.

If this doesn't work out, I will be devastated. I can't go there. Doing so, will only make it happen. For now, I'll stay present and enjoy every bit of this newfound companionship.

"See ya later," he whispers, leaving me all sorts of fluttery.

He passes Charlie and she holds up a hand. "Hey, Jerome."

As usual, she's dressed to the teeth in a navy pencil skirt, pale blue blouse and stilettos that would make me snap an ankle. Sunlight glistens over her blonde hair and I take a second to glance at my cut-off jean shorts and ripped AC/DC concert shirt.

Hard to believe the two of us came from the same gene pool.

"Good morning," I say. "What's up?"

Generally, Charlie doesn't check in on me in the morning. She prefers to not waste time and heads straight to the office where I eventually roll in.

Her presence now indicates something must've popped overnight regarding a case.

Leather briefcase in hand, she pauses in front of her car, leaning one hip against it. "Alfonzo."

"The FBI guy you hired?"

She lets out a sarcastic grunt. "I may be rescinding that offer."

Oh, interesting. Charlie is an ace when it comes to vetting people, not to mention her dedication to standing by her word, so if she's bailing on an offer there must be something seriously naughty hiding in this guy's closet.

I move closer, as if we're about to share top-secret info. "Why is that?"

"I've received intel I don't like."

"From JJ?"

She cocks her head, but stays silent, reminding me of our rule that she won't share what he tells her. Some call it pillow talk. Charlie prefers intel.

"Sorry," I say. "Forgot I'm not supposed to ask."

She waves it away. "Baez maybe dirty."

Whoa. "Seriously? You missed that?"

In response, I receive the Charlie Schock death glare. It wouldn't be the first time she's drilled me with her pretty azure eyes, but it's still enough to make my bladder weak.

"Really, Meg? That's what you're going with?"

Shame churns inside me, making my cheeks hot. "I'm sorry," I blurt. "I didn't mean it in a rude way. I'm just... surprised. You normally flag that stuff."

"Tough to catch this one. The AG started an internal investigation into how Al and his partner were able to close cases so fast. And then a key witness, who was going to give the proof they needed to dig deeper, went AWOL."

"And he still had a job?"

"Not exactly. The Bureau didn't have enough evidence, but the rumor is they encouraged him to retire early. If he took the deal, they'd bury the investigation. It allowed him to keep his reputation—and commendations—intact."

I let out a low whistle and Charlie spends the next few minutes filling me in on an informant who accused Alfonzo of entrapment. The entire thing sounds way too sordid for Schock Investigations, so I don't blame Charlie for waffling on hiring the guy.

Employment status with our agency aside, our mother has aligned herself with this man. "Mom thinks the world of him."

"I know. Which is why I'm going to excavate every secret he has. We need to know who—and what—we're dealing with." She slides her strap to her shoulder and pulls her keys from the front pocket. "She was planning to come in and make some calls this morning, but she's got a migraine. You're off the hook. You still coming in?"

I gaze off at a passing car. Our neighbor two doors down with the yappy dog. We exchange a wave and I go back to Charlie. "I was thinking I'd ride out to Mom and Dad's. Maybe stop by Marie's." I circle my hand around my head. "Something isn't sitting right about her. I can check on Mom while I'm there."

"Your instincts are good, so if you feel like you need to explore it, have at it."

"I keep thinking about this FBI most wanted angle and all those paintings. She's been a lot of places."

"Maybe she likes to travel."

Charlie playing devil's advocate. Something she enjoys when we're hashing out cases.

"Perhaps. But if we're going to get Mom to back off, I want to satisfy myself. So, I'm off for a visit where I'll stop and purchase one of the paintings I saw on Marie's website. Windswept. Which, by the way, is a horrible name for a painting of a lighthouse."

At that, Charlie chuckles. She heads to the driver's side of her shiny BMW that glistens under a perfect morning sun. "Check in when you're done. Let me know what you've found."

Ninety minutes later, after showering and dressing in a fresh pair of jeans and my favorite tie-dyed T-shirt, I park in front of my parents' and text mom, letting her know I'm doing reconnaissance and she should not, under any circumstances, make an appearance.

Gayle and Marie already know she's spying. Marie made that clear at the art fair. Mom showing up while I'm buying a painting won't help our cause.

I spot an SUV along with an older model Toyota—Gayle's car. Damn. I was hoping to catch Marie alone, but whatever.

Winging it has never been an issue for me, something that irritates the hell out of Charlie.

I stride up the walkway, keeping my pace casual in case they have one of those cameras everyone is chattering about. I sure as heck don't want to appear nervous or up to something. Nope. Not me. Just a friendly neighbor stopping in for a chat.

As I approach, I draw in a breath, easing it out slowly while I punch the doorbell.

A few seconds later, the door opens and I'm greeted by

Marie in a pair of paint-stained hospital scrubs. Her long hair is in a ponytail and her right cheek marred with a smudge of black.

Clearly, I've caught her at work.

"Hello," she says, her eyes brightening.

"Hi, Marie. I'm sorry to barge in on you." I gesture to my parents' home. "I was visiting and wanted to see if you still had Windswept available. I saw it on your website."

Her jaw drops and I'm left to wonder if her shock is over my willingness to buy her stuff or the fact I've shown up at her door to do so. Maybe both.

"Windswept?"

"I'd like to buy it. Is it available?"

A wide, open-mouthed smile splits her face. "Oh, my goodness. Yes. Of course I have it. I can't believe you want it."

I let out a soft laugh. "Um, Marie? No offense, but you need to fix your sales strategy."

She slaps her hands over her cheeks and a sharp stab of guilt guts me. This woman thinks I really want to own her work. As an artist, I know that rush. That euphoric moment when someone loves your creation enough to sacrifice their hard-earned money for it.

Marie drops her hands and straightens her shoulders. "You're so right. I'm just...excited. I mean, after we met, I looked you up. You're an accomplished artist. And your reconstructions? They're amazing. I could learn so much from you. Why would you want my painting?"

Not only am I scamming this woman, she's complimenting me. Excellent. Still, I manage to give her an aw-shucks smile I pray hides my deception. "Well, thank you. But don't sell yourself short. You're work has a...vibe...to it. Embrace it."

Again, guilt plunges its mighty sword into my chest. I'll need five—maybe six—pot brownies after this.

She nods and points toward the garage. "I have them in there."

I follow while refraining from schooling her on proper climate-controlled storage. We're not talking about a Monet here, but still, dampness is murder on art.

We reach the garage and Marie huddles close to the keypad on the outside, blocking my view as she punches in the code.

Dang. That would've been a nice get, but again, who knew what kind of security Gayle had installed. The way my luck is running lately, he'd catch us on camera searching his home.

The door slowly rises, the chain squeaking enough to be annoying. Or maybe that's the guilt again, scraping against my last set of nerves.

Marie waits for the door to complete its ascent and waves me to follow her into an orderly two-car garage with a rear entry along the back wall. My parents have the same. Comes in handy for yardwork.

Half of this particular garage is definitely the man cave, complete with a long bench and one of those giant, bright red tool chests. In the middle of the floor sits various woodworking projects; a table, two broken chairs, a hutch.

"Gayle likes to rescue furniture from the trash and refurbish it," Marie says.

I shove my hands straight into my pockets. All I can think about is the bad energy that accompanies used furniture. How the hell do they know someone's head didn't get chopped off on that table?

So not touching that stuff.

"This," Marie spreads her arms wide, "is my half."

Against the back wall are four rows of blank canvasses, all arranged by size. On the side are slim boxes of varying heights. At least she's wrapped the paintings and has them vertical. She's not a total loss when it comes to proper storage.

Another two dozen paintings are lined up against the wall, these unwrapped, but also upright.

I bite my lip, determined not to lecture her.

She moves to one end of the row of unwrapped paintings. "I think Windswept is in here. Otherwise, it's in the boxes."

I glance at the opposite end and my opportunity to see what exactly she has. "How about I start there? It'll be faster if we both look."

"Sure," she chirps. "You know what you're searching for, so go ahead."

I do so, eyeing more lighthouses, a couple bridges and... whoa, I halt at the seventh.

A woman in front of an old-fashioned ice cream parlor with the swirly font on the plate glass window. Inside, I imagine there are counter stools where locals enjoy a sugar cone dripping with butter pecan. Or a hot-fudged sundae drizzled with what my father calls wet walnuts.

The woman though is the real scene stealer and it has nothing to do with her appearance. She is, in fact, quite unremarkable. Shoulder length, muddy brown hair parted down the middle, a thick nose and narrow lips. She's not ugly, just...average.

However, every painting of Marie's I've seen is a landscape.

Zero people.

Ever.

Except this dark-haired woman. Which makes her an attention-stealer.

"Did you find it?"

This from Marie who steps closer so I shake my head. "No." I lift the painting from the row. "But this is fabulous."

She tilts her head, staring at it a few seconds while the hairs on my neck dance and my mind spins theories on who the woman is. Friend? Sister? Mother?

Random nobody?

I glance at Marie, who stares at the painting. Nothing about her body language tells me anything. No longing in her eyes or wistful sigh, but there's an uneasiness. Something deep and...painful.

For whatever reason, and I have to assume it's the woman, I get the feeling this piece is important to her.

"Where is this?"

Marie straightens and heads toward me. "Oh, that's nothing."

Gently, she takes it from me, placing it back in the row. "It's an early one. I'm terrible at portraits so I gave up."

She returns to the row of paintings while I consider ways to get her talking again.

"Here it is!" Marie swings it toward me. "Windswept!" I paste a faux smile on my face. She points at the lower, rear corner where she's written something on the wood frame just beyond the edge of the canvas. "And, just so you know, I add the name to the back. See," she says, "Windswept." She spins it again. "This is the one you wanted, right?"

I nod, but my mind is on the portrait she'd taken out of my hands. "That's it," I say. "And now that I've seen the other, I'll take it, too. How much for both?"

Slowly, her mouth drifts open and she stands there, apparently gobsmacked by my offer. "Marie?"

"That not for sale. Just Windswept."

Damn. "Are you sure? I'd be happy to pay extra."

She shakes her head a little too hard and takes a teensy step back. I'm spooking her.

Which only fuels my curiosity.

"No," she says, her voice carrying a hard edge.

An absolute warning that I should back off and regroup.

"All right. But, if you change your mind, I'd love to have it."

I dig into my pocket where I stashed the amount I saw on Marie's website. "Here you go. One hundred twenty-five, right?"

She takes the bills, but returns the twenty and the five. "Just one hundred, since you came out here and all."

For a second, I consider protesting, but decide against it. Why squabble and make more out of a simple transaction than necessary? I hold up the cash. "Thank you for the discount."

I take the painting from her and head toward the door, my mind focused on figuring out another way to get a look at the portrait I've left behind.

And the name on the back of it.

11

Charlie

The heat index is over a hundred by the time I reach the office. I park in front under the single tree, leaving the rear parking lot's shade for Meg when she arrives. I wrestle with my briefcase, lock the Beemer, and walk inside to find Haley with an oscillating fan fluttering papers on her desk. Her cheeks are flushed. It's cooler in the building than outside, but not by much.

"Did it finally quit?" I ask.

She doesn't look up from her typing. "Not yet, but it's on its last leg. I already called the A/C guys. They'll be here Friday."

"That's the soonest they can work on it?"

She nods, stops typing, and holds out two pink message slips to me. "And before you ask, I've already called the others in the area and they're all booked as well. Half of the tri-state area is suffering from the heat."

Reluctantly, I take the slips. "Thanks. If you get too hot, you can work from home."

She resumes typing. "It's only seventy-six in here, and Matt brought these fans. I'm fine."

My blouse is already sticking to my skin. I walk down the hall and our resident fan hero meets me before I reach my door. He's dressed for the warm day, a bright blue button-down short sleeve shirt matching his eyes.

"Got the pictures you wanted. Shouldn't be an issue for Mrs. Olsen to proceed with whatever she's going to do about her marriage. The file is on the desk."

One case closed. I salute him. "Thank you for doing that."

He follows me and I see a large coffee waiting on my desk. How did Meg and I get so lucky to have him? "Did you have to stay out all night?"

"Three hours," he says with the cavalierness of an investigator. He plops in the chair and kicks his feet out. "I've had worse."

Since he's wearing an *I've got a secret* look on his face, and the fact he's still sitting here, I assume there's more to the story. Or maybe he wants to work from home as well, thanks to our failing air conditioner. "Appreciate you bringing in the fans." I walk to the new one on my credenza and punch the low button.

"Bought them with petty cash."

Ah, not as heroic, but still appreciated. "Surprised there was enough in there."

"You probably should refill the funds."

I turn to the desk and reach for the coffee. "Shouldn't be a problem once Olsen pays up."

"There's an interesting twist to her case," he says, and sure enough, when I glance at him, a grin spreads across his face.

"Spill it."

"Mr. Olsen's girlfriend is sister to Patty Belkin."

My brain stutters for a second, then makes the connection.

"The Patty Belkin I'm investigating for embezzling at Markent Corp?"

He nods, still grinning like a kid with his hand in the cookie jar. "I did a background check and I think you'll find it interesting. Seems the sisters have quite an enterprise going."

He launches to his feet, taps the folder he's placed on my desk. "If you get the goods on Patty, you shouldn't have any problem closing that case by the end of the day as well with the information I dug up. They particularly enjoy funding trips to Vegas and Miami."

He winks and leaves.

"I love you, Matt," I call. I'm due at Markent Corp in two hours. Patty's boss alerted me she called in sick today, so I'm installing tracking software on her computer to see how and where she's diverting funds.

"Love you, too, boss," he calls back.

By the end of today, I could have two cases closed. I sip the coffee—no amount of heat keeps me away from the stuff—and prepare for the meeting I've set up with Al.

I tend to confront problems head on, and the behind-the-scenes investigation on Al before he quit the Bureau is not something I can dance around. I need to rescind my offer, even if I don't call him on the carpet about it. I haven't yet decided whether to throw that in his face or not, but I'm sure he'll want to know why I've had a change of heart.

When he arrives fifteen minutes later, Haley shows him to my office, and I still haven't decided whether I'm going to bring it up.

His shirt looks freshly pressed, as do his khakis, the humidity seeming not to bother him. His cologne is fragrant but light enough to not be overwhelming. He leans across the desk to shake my hand, eyes the fan, and takes a seat in the chair Matt vacated. "This heat is something, isn't it?"

He gives me a smile that I don't return. "Thank you for coming in on short notice."

"I've given your offer extensive consideration, and I'm ready to start work whenever you need me. Have you had a break in your mother's case?"

I haven't heard from Meg and her fishing expedition yet, and with Mom down with a migraine, I don't expect to. Thank God. "I'm afraid I have to rescind that offer."

His face falls, eyes widening with surprise. "I'm sorry to hear that. Is something wrong?"

I decide to go with a generic answer, always a safe option. "After considering it, I decided there's too much conflict of interest. Mom hired us, and she's in the group with you. We're not exactly unbiased, and at this point, I feel it would be safer to keep you out of our investigation so you remain on the unbiased side of things."

He tilts his head, frowning, as if wondering where this is coming from. Then he takes a deep breath, expanding his broad chest, and sighs loudly. He looks away, runs a hand over his face and nods as if I've caught him in a lie.

Maybe I have.

The FBI trained me to be a profiler. It came naturally. His body language suggests he's either relieved or trying to hide a secret. Most would rush to continue the conversation, but I learned a long time ago that patience is one of the best tools in my toolbox.

As if he's made a decision, his gaze returns to mine. "She knows, doesn't she?"

He seems to be talking about Mom. Does he realize I discovered the internal investigation? Does he think I've told her? Again, I stare back and say nothing.

Silence tends to make people talk. Even former agents. But I don't expect what he says next. "I thought I hid it well enough, but I'm sure she picked up on it." He shakes his head with a sad expression. "She's a beautiful, intelligent woman. You can't blame me for falling for her."

I try not to let my mouth drop open.

He continues. "It's just...she loves the hunt, like I do. I've not run into many women who are as caught up in the mystery and suspense of hunting down serial killers as she is."

He pauses as if he wants me to confirm this is an exceptional thing in a woman. I'm so stunned I can't react.

"You know how it is," he continues.

I'm sure I don't.

He gives a half-hearted smile. "She's got that spark. That need to find the truth. It's what drives all of us, but I've never met anyone quite like her before."

I try not to flinch or draw back, even though inside I'm doing both. Strike one—the AG's office was doing an internal investigation on Al before he retired. Strike two—he thinks he's in love with my mother.

Definitely rescinding the job offer.

For one of the few times in my life, words continue to escape me. Meg would say I'm flashing my resting bitch face, but honestly, I'm just working to keep all expression off it.

He leans forward in the seat, eyes pleading. "I swear, I would never act on my feelings. She's made it quite clear she's happily married, and I respect that. Our relationship has always been completely professional."

I force a nod and find my voice. "Good to know."

He stands, flustered, and focuses on the fan again. "I understand about the job. No problem. But please, let me know if there's anything I can help with when it comes to the case. I know you probably won't reach out, but I want you to know, I'm here if you need anything."

I simply stare, holding in a curse, a threat, and my complete irritation over this conversation. He seems to take the hint, raises his hand in goodbye, and vacates the room.

Before I can regroup, Meg arrives in a flurry. Flying down the hallway, she hollers a good morning at Matt, and bursts into my office. She's grinning from ear to ear and I wonder how her little buying spree went.

"You're not gonna believe what just happened," I say.

"I think I have something on Marie," she states, at the same time.

I shake myself to rid the idea of Alfonzo being sweet on our mother. Shifting gears, I motion her forward. "What?"

She tosses her tote bag into the chair and paces. From her mouth spills the details of her morning visit. The painting of the woman. The name she is sure is on the back of the canvas.

"And how does that tie in with the serial killer angle?"

"No idea," she says, undaunted, "but there's something there. A secret she's hiding. We need to get inside and check the back of that painting."

Everybody has secrets. Not all of them are connected to crimes. "How do you propose we do that? Please tell me you're not gonna make me buy one of those ugly lighthouses."

She's still pacing, not looking at me now, her mind a thousand miles away. Or maybe just twenty, back in Marie and Gayle's garage. She taps a finger on her chin. "I'm thinking about it. I have a plan."

Matt strolls in, and I swear it's because he has a nose for excitement. "Whatever it is, I'm in if it's gets us out of the building."

Meg chuckles and goes to stand by the fan, holding her arms up where sweat has pooled under them. "Did you know Gayle refinishes furniture?"

My morning has been entirely disjointed; I rub my temples where I feel a headache brewing at this left turn in the conversation. Mom may not be the only one with a migraine.

"I can't believe people are so into that," she continues without waiting for an answer.

Matt props his hands on the back of a chair. "What's wrong with it? Taylor loves some of that stuff. She's always making me go to that shop off the interstate with the chubby chic stuff. The owner buys antiques and paints them."

"*Shabby* chic," Meg corrects. "You never know what kind of energy you're picking up. Who knows what's been done on those tables, or in those chairs?"

My sister has a thing about energy and transference between people and things. Matt just glances at me and lifts his brows.

"We've seen many violent crime scenes," I tell him. "Lots of blood and other...you know. Tables, chairs, couches, beds, you name it, they've either been used as weapons, or have caught the brunt of violence that occurred."

Meg's nodding. "Remember the trunk you found when you were still at the Bureau? The one with the bones in it of that missing teenage girl?"

It's a case I'll never forget, although I wish I could. "What better way to get rid of DNA evidence than to strip furniture and refurbish it."

At this, Matt appears mildly contemplative. "Maybe Gayle is a serial and that's why he refinishes furniture."

Meg whirls to stare at me, as if Matt just shed light on a whole new convincing angle. "Oh my God, Matt's right."

Either the heat or this morning's revelations are starting to make me dizzy. I motion at Meg to move away from the fan so I can get more air.

"Let's put that on the back burner for the moment." I need to make sure my little sister isn't going to do something crazy, ranking up there with our mother. "What's your plan to get a look at the back of that canvas?"

She claps her hands and rubs them together. There's a gleam in her eye and I have a sneaking suspicion I'm not going to like it. "We,"—she points at me then back at herself—"are gonna get in there when they're gone and have a good look at that portrait."

Now, I'm the one who needs clarification to make sure I'm on the right train. "You want to break into Gayle's garage to see the name on a canvas Marie painted?"

"Yes!"

I glance at Matt for confirmation she sounds like a lunatic, but he straightens and stretches his arms overhead. "I'll be the lookout. How will we know when they're gone?"

My head pounds. "You can't be serious. We can't do a B and E on Gayle's garage."

Meg and Matt ignore my protest, excited, like we're going to their favorite restaurant for lunch. "I'm onto something," Meg says. "I can feel it, Charlie. I don't know about the serial killer stuff, but Marie and these paintings? That portrait? It's fishy."

She faces Matt. "Mom's watching the house. Gayle is already out, and she's gonna call if she sees Marie leave."

Matt checks his watch, sauntering to the door. "Alert me when you get the word, but we really should wait until dark, regardless of whether they're home or not."

He walks out, leaving me and my sister to look at each other. "You think I'm crazy, don't you?" she accuses.

At this point, I'm starting to think the whole world is, and it's not just because of the heat. "If we're doing this, I'm gonna have to change," I tell her. "And Matt's right. We wait until dark and the two of you will do exactly what I tell you to. Got it?"

The expression on her face, and the smile she gives me, is priceless.

12

Meg

Three people dressed in black is never good. In my mind, it means a funeral or an amateur break-in.

In our case, given that it's one in the morning, it's the latter. Well, in my case, at least. Charlie, I'm not sure about. My sister is ballsy. I could see her popping a lock every now and again and helping herself into a residence.

Matt?

He's definitely a pro. He calls these events sneak-n-peeks. I'm not sure how comfortable I am with his casual attitude regarding burglary, but whatever. It's not for me to worry about.

Frankly, he should be the one going inside rather than being the lookout, but I know which painting we want and where it's stored so we've made the joint decision it'll be faster if I go in with Charlie.

"You ready?" Matt asks from behind the wheel of my minivan.

79

My parents' street is dark, lit only by the quaint lamps that sporadically dot the parkways. Zero traffic from either direction.

Before tonight, I hadn't realized it was an absolute welcoming committee for burglars—or worse. After we complete this, I'm writing a letter to the town council insisting on better lighting. Our parents are getting older and although Cedarwood Cove is safe, you never know.

From the passenger seat, a line of pricklies marches straight up my neck. What the hell am I doing? This was my idea, one I was excited about, but I've had all day to consider it and too much thinking tends to make me squirrelly. I'm an artist for God's sakes and I'm about to commit a felony.

Sure, it's only a fourth degree in Maryland—I checked—but it could earn us three years and I have no intention of becoming someone's prison bitch. That, I couldn't handle.

Charlie?

She'd carve someone's eye out with a toilet paper shiv and become boss.

Me?

Toast.

When I don't answer, Matt glances at me. "Meg?"

I nod. "As much as I can be, I guess. Charlie?"

"Yep."

Of course she is. She's always ready.

Matt eases up on the gas pedal as he nears the corner. "I'll drop you here and circle the block." He points out the windshield. "I'll park in front of that house."

The Jenkinsons' home.

"That's good," Charlie responds. "They're old and go to bed at nine. You won't have any pain in the ass nosey-bodies wondering what you're doing."

"Well, aside from Mom," I add because she loves nothing

more than sitting in her front window at night and spying on her quirky neighbor.

"Don't worry about her," Charlie says as if she's reading a damned grocery list. "I told her if she saw anything suspicious at Gayle's not to call the cops."

I whip around and gawk at my sister. "You told her?"

"Uh, yeah."

The holier-than-thou voice. Excellent.

"Hey." She waggles her hand. "You know how she is. If she saw anything, she'd call 911, then we'd all have to explain why we're breaking into our neighbor's garage. Wouldn't that be fun?"

I see the logic, but...Mom? Really? "I thought she had a migraine."

"She did. She slept all day and feels better."

Which meant, she'd be up half the night trying to get her cycle back on track. And when Mom couldn't sleep, she got busy.

Watching Gayle.

"Damn."

Charlie, always one to relish being right, tugs her black skull cap over her head, tucking her ponytail up inside it. "You can thank me later when the cops don't throw us in the clink."

Oh, ha, ha.

In front of the Jenkinsons', Matt pulls to the side of the road. "Go. Make it fast. No snooping around. Both cars are in the driveway. They're probably sleeping." He glances toward the house. "The place isn't that big and it's old. Paper thin walls probably. If you're in there too long, they'll hear you."

The more he talks, the more my stomach cramps. I'm so not ready for this.

I pull my own cap on and offer a salute. "Sir, yes, sir."

"Don't take the painting. Just snap photos. Get in and get out. They won't even know you were there."

MISTY EVANS & ADRIENNE GIORDANO

Charlie muscles the side door of my ancient van open and hops out. "That's the plan. Let's go, Meg."

"I'll pretend the engine is dead or something," Matt says. "Keep your phones handy. If there's any heat, I'll text."

We move away, keeping closer to the homes and away from the street lights. Humidity thickens the night air and clogs my lungs. I draw a few deep breaths, but it all feels ominous to me. Like the heat and quiet are warning us to stay away. To run.

Then again, I'm a wuss and more than likely freaking myself out.

Gayle's house is the second in from the corner so we hook a right and cut through his neighbor's yard. The area is gleefully dark and unfenced, allowing us to move quickly to the back door of the garage.

Charlie slides two pairs of gloves from her lightweight shoulder pack and hands one over. Now we're getting serious. Next, she digs out a penlight and shines it on the doorknob.

"No deadbolt," she whispers. "Easy."

My sister, the cat burglar. Go figure. I'm equal parts horrified and wildly impressed she can be so calm when we're about to bust open a lock.

She points at the penlight, then to the knob, letting me know what she wants me to do. We're actually doing this. Now that we're here, I'm starting to chicken out.

Worse, my pulse is racing, my heart banging against my chest so hard it's all I can focus on.

Stop.

If I don't, my nerves will take over and I'll be assailed by a panic attack that'll blow this whole thing. These are not uncommon for me. Thus, the pot brownies. Since I've started my little weed regimen, I've managed to keep them limited to one every few months.

Or in times of high stress.

Not that a B and E with my sister is stressful or anything. And, oh my God, the clunk of a jail cell closing fills my head.

Sensing my hesitation, Charlie looks at me, then gets right next to my ear. "You're fine. Take a breath and focus on my voice. We'll be out of here in two minutes. I promise. All I need is for you to hold the light. Now, don't fuck this up."

My sister. The Queen of Sensitivity.

But she knows me well enough to know that's exactly what I needed to snap my mind to attention.

I draw a deep breath, snatch it from her and aim it at the doorknob while I check our surroundings. Everything is still dark. Halfway down the road, a small, second floor window— probably a bathroom—is illuminated.

Nothing I can do except pray they don't look out and see an odd light in Gayle's yard.

When it goes dark again, I let out a long breath and return my focus to Charlie who is holding a small leather pouch.

She flips it open, grabbing what looks like some kind of metal tool and a pick before shoving the pouch in her pack again.

My continued amazement at my sister's lock picking skills expands as she inserts the tool into the keyhole, maneuvers it and turns it clockwise then counterclockwise. Still holding the wrench thingy, she guides the pick into the lock, then repeats the process several times until...boom...she turns the knob and we're in.

Just that fast. Wow.

I blink twice and my pulse kicks again, but it's not panic this time.

Holy crap. My sister is good. I shove around Charlie, keeping the penlight pointed downward so I don't trip on anything. Once I reach the rack of paintings on the far wall, I clasp the penlight between my teeth and force myself not to think about all the places that sucker may have been and the germs that come with it.

Then Charlie is next to me, removing it and pointing it at the line of canvases.

Focus, focus, focus.

Marie placed the painting somewhere in the middle so I pick a random canvas in that general location.

Nope.

Next one.

Lighthouse.

Not it.

Next.

Rock formation.

Dammit. Did she move it? Or worse, sell it?

Just as I start to believe this is a wasted exercise that'll surely land us in orange jumpsuits...there it is.

Yes!

My mind explodes. I need my phone. Back pocket. I reach for it and with my free hand jab a finger at the painting. Charlie grips the edge, starts to slide it out and bumps the one next to it. A thud no louder than a pebble hitting grass sounds, but in the quiet of the garage it might as well be a bomb going off.

Hurry, hurry, hurry.

I snap three photos of the front, wait for Charlie to whip it around and...*thank you, thank you*...there's a name on the wooden frame.

Evelyn.

Something tickles my mind, but I'm too excited. Too strung out to focus on any one thing. I'll think about it later.

I quickly check the pictures, zooming in to make sure they're clear, then bob my head. Using great care this time, Charlie returns the painting to its spot and jerks her head toward the door.

Where our mother is standing.

13

Charlie

*M*eg sucks in a startled breath and I whip my head around. Standing in the doorway, hands on hips, is the last person I'd hoped to see tonight—outside of Gayle or Marie.

Moonlight creates a backdrop behind her, the beam of my flashlight skimming over her face. "Did you find it?" Mom asks in a stage whisper.

Meg's gasp made my stomach drop and my pulse skyrocket. Now, I take a slow, quiet breath to regain my composure. This is not the place to have a conversation, and, as I motion her outside, I grab my phone and text Matt.

You're fired.

I've already started toward the door, but Mom is blocking it. "Well, did you?"

I move into her personal space, glaring as I lean in close to her ear. "We need to leave now," I whisper.

My phone vibrates silently in my hand. Matt. His text is slightly panicky.

What??? Why?

Mom's not moving and Meg is on my heels. I grip our mother by the arm and gently steer her out the door.

Before we get two steps, I hear voices. Someone's feet hit the floor as if they're getting out of bed.

Shit. By the heavy footsteps, I'm sure it's Gayle.

The steps head across the floor, and I hear a murmured voice—his.

Meg touches my lower back, as if rushing me to push Mom out the door. My pulse jackrabbits as my mind considers our options.

We need to move, but I can't take them across the backyard, in case Gayle or Marie looks out. We have to cling to the shadows, avoiding the blue-gray moonlight, or risk raising an alarm.

I pocket my phone and grab Meg's hand. Very softly in the distance, I hear a door opening and closing. I sneak a glance over my shoulder and cringe. The strip at the bottom of the door leading into the house—and what I suspect is the kitchen —is illuminated with light.

Double shit.

With a strong nudge, I force Mom out and pull Meg behind me. Maintaining silence, I physically stack both of them against the outside garage wall, and, quick as a cat, close the exterior door as silently as possible.

Meg and I kill our flashlights, but I can see her and Mom's faces with ease, thanks to the annoyingly bright moon. I hold a finger to my lips, and sure enough, a light comes on in the garage, shining through the tiny window above us.

Blood rushes in my ears. Not fear, per se, but annoyance.

How I long for my bed, cool air conditioning, the feel of JJ's body next to mine...

I wonder what the hell I'm doing here. It was fun to bring

Meg and Matt on this expedition, but this is serious, and we are literally footsteps away from being discovered.

If it was just me, I'd stay in the shadows of the house until I got to the hedge and be out of here in a heartbeat. Because I'm not alone, I have to make wise choices in the coming seconds.

If Gayle looks out, he'll see us. There's no way I can explain what we're doing—to him or the police. I crouch, meeting Meg and Mom's eyes, and motioning them to do the same. They watch me like deer caught in headlights, and as I move to the front of our conga line, both of them respond.

Careful not to trip over anything at my feet, I tiptoe with slow, careful steps, keeping close to the house until we round the backside. There, I drop to hands and knees to go under one of the windows, past the back porch, and under a second window.

Pausing, I double check to make sure Mom and Meg catch up. Like good soldiers, they mimic everything I do.

In the pause, I listen carefully to sounds coming from inside the house. We're in the shadows by the far corner. The driveway is a wide strip of moonlight between the house and hedge.

I stay frozen for so long, I feel Mom tug my ankle. I ignore her.

My whole focus is on getting them across that driveway safely, the hedge a mere four feet away, but in between is that spotlight from the moon.

Looking up, I eye the house for any signs of light, other than illumination coming from the kitchen. After several seconds, I'm rewarded when the window falls dark again, Gayle flicking off the overhead light.

Relief surges through me and then Mom pinches my leg hard. I look back over my shoulder, still in my doggy position, to glare at her. She motions with her hand, as if to say *let's go*.

I still can't believe she showed up after I explicitly made her

MISTY EVANS & ADRIENNE GIORDANO

promise not to interfere. A part of me, on the other hand, isn't surprised at all. I thought I was circumventing this very situation, but maybe it was stupid to let her in on our plans. Of course, she couldn't resist.

Waiting out Gayle is tougher than I expect, only because Mom is so impatient. My phone vibrates in my pocket, Matt once more trying to figure out what's wrong. When all I hear are crickets and the sound of a night creature moving in the hedge, I do another scan of the windows. No one is looking out, and only then do I motion Mom and Meg to cross the great divide of moonlight.

Once they're safe on the other side and no alarm has been raised, I cross the drive myself. Twenty steps later, we all jump into Meg's van and Matt releases a loud sigh of relief.

"What the hell?" he asks, looking at our mother.

"What the hell is right." I whirl in the passenger seat to glare at her. She and Meg are arranging themselves in the back, Meg shoving some folded-up canvasses out of the way so Mom has a spot to sit.

Mom looks at me as if she doesn't understand. "Did you find it or not?"

"I specifically told you not to interfere," I say, grinding my teeth. To Matt, "Let's go."

He puts the van in gear and takes off.

She huffs. "I wasn't interfering, but I didn't know what was taking so long. You said you'd text me as soon as you were done."

Meg says in a very patient voice, "We weren't done, Mom."

She leaves out the word *obviously* but it hangs in the air. I turn up the air conditioning and adjust the vent to blow directly on me. I'm sweating like a pig, not just from the heat.

"That kind of operation takes time and finesse," I state.

I'm impressed by Meg's continued patience. "We did get the

name of the woman, and I took a picture," she tells our mother. "Let's get you home. I, for one, could use a cold drink."

Mom doesn't even seem to register what she's said. "I have a bone to pick with you, Charlie."

Seriously?

I don't reply, once again wondering how my life jumped the normal tracks.

Matt takes the alley to my parents' place, headlights flashing on the back of the house. "Does Dad know you're running around in the middle of the night?" I ask.

As she bails out the side door with Meg, Mom says, "He's still on his fishing trip."

In a way, that's good. I follow her inside, Matt bringing up the rear. We file into the kitchen, and Meg goes for a glass of water. I wish for something stronger.

Mom stands at the counter and taps a fingernail on the marble. "I just got off the phone with Alfonzo. He told me you fired him."

"Technically, I never hired him. I made an offer, then thought better of it. It's nothing personal."

"Why would you do that?" From her expression, it's *very* personal. "He was looking forward to helping and working on this investigation."

I debate telling her the truth, but I can't share the information about the internal investigation, nor do I plan to tell her he has a crush on her.

Matt has taken several steps back, pulled out his phone, and is acting as though he's not part of this conversation. Meg sips her water and watches the match between me and Mom with a humorous glint in her eyes.

"It's best for all of us. We need someone who is detached from the outcome, that understands the legal and forensic side of serial killers, but isn't emotionally involved." I offer the same excuse I used on him. "The best thing for you is to avoid conflict of interest, and unfortunately, if I hire Al to work on the case, we definitely have that."

She screws up her lips in a classic thinking-it-over pose.

Good. I continue. "Meg and I are directly related to you, so there's already an issue there. We could skew our theories and ideas simply because we want to make you happy. I need someone outside of the family and Schock Investigations to give us a nonbiased viewpoint if anything crucial comes up. Do you understand?"

I see the gears in her head turning, her mind searching for someplace to attack. She unscrews her lips. "He doesn't have anybody, Charlie. He has the volunteer work with the citizen's group. That's it. When you offered him a job, you can't imagine how happy he was. I want him on the case. If not, then give him something else to work on, but don't take the job away."

Meg looks at me with a weighted expression. Distraction is my only hope. "Why were you talking to Al at one in the morning?"

Mom's brows dip. "What does that have to do with anything?"

She's hedging. My stomach drops a little, wondering if she might have a tiny crush on him, too. "I'm curious. Dad's gone and you're talking to another guy in the middle of the night?"

She rolls her eyes dramatically and laughs off the veiled accusation. "For your information, Al created a private Facebook group for the committee where we share things about different cases. We brainstorm. He and I often have trouble sleeping, and tonight, I saw he was online and messaged him. I wanted to see how his first day with you went." Her brows go back up and she shoots me an accusing look. "He said you fired him before he even got started. Of course, I wanted to know what was going on, so I called him."

"And what did he say?" Meg asks before I can.

"He quoted the same baloney Charlie just spat out."

She leans forward, once more her face pleading. "He told me he'd do pro bono work if that's what it takes just to have his fingers back in the investigating pie. He misses it, and he really likes you two. Isn't there anything you can give him to make him happy again?"

There's no arguing with her, and I'm tired. The adrenaline rush is fading. I long for a glass of wine and JJ's hands on my neck and shoulders, massaging away the tension.

"I'll figure something out," I tell her. Not a promise, not a lie.

Meg shoots me another look, a question mark behind her gaze. I shrug.

Taking a few steps forward, I kiss Mom on the cheek. "What are you doing tomorrow? Do you want to come by the office and help us?"

"I'm...busy."

Meg has moved in to give our mother a hug, as well, but this stops her in her tracks. "With what?"

"I have a lunch date." She glances away, then back to us. "With a friend."

It doesn't take a genius to jump to the conclusion she's going out with Al. I don't like it, but she's an adult, and that's another argument I'm not up for.

I give her arm a squeeze and round up Matt. "We'll call if we figure out who the woman is in the portrait," I say, motioning him toward the door. He looks relieved.

"Have you done anything else on the case?" Mom asks, and it seems directed at me.

I stop and face her, drawing from Meg's well of patience. "I spent three hours this afternoon on it. I contacted the medical examiner in Grayson County, who still has the bones of the unidentified woman. I requested a DNA sample and they turned me down, since I'm not law enforcement or family. In reality, they don't have the budget to take samples from unclaimed bones or the manpower to constantly recheck databases."

Another tangent of mine that's unnecessary to get into right now. "So I called my contact at the Attorney General's office"—everyone knows that's JJ—"and he put heat on them. Found out a sample had already been taken and ran through a database years ago. They're sending the analysis from that original test, plus a new genetic sample to my friend tomorrow. Once we have all that, we can run it through Family Ties, as well as uploading it to GenCo, and maybe we'll get a hit, some distant relative."

"Oh," Mom says, pleasantly surprised.

"I also left messages for family members of the women who were identified and I'm waiting for responses from them," I continue. "I've been through Alfonzo's case notes, which I already told him how much I appreciated, and I have a couple other leads to check into."

This seems to satisfy her and she nods. "Thank you."

I give her a weary smile and she returns it over Meg's shoulder as my sister hugs her. "We'll talk tomorrow," Meg says.

She and Matt follow me out to the van. Matt shakes his head as he starts it and backs down the driveway. "I can't believe she showed up at the garage."

I glance at Meg and she puts her hands to her head in mock horror. "That's our Mom," she says.

As Matt pulls onto the road, I look toward Gayle and Marie's, relieved to see there are no lights on, no commotion, no police cars. "I have the uneasy feeling that whatever Mom and Alfonzo are doing involves more than lunch," I say.

"Like what?" Meg asks.

I glance at Matt. "How would you like to tail our mom?"

"I thought I was fired."

Smartass.

He flashes a grin and makes a whatever motion. "You're the boss," he says. "If you want me to follow Mama Schock, then that's what I'll do."

14

Meg

My mood matches a bleary gray sky. This morning I'm battling several things. My lack of sleep and blown routine, which, for a girl who likes to keep to a ten pm to six am sleep cycle, could be dangerous.

I'm off-kilter today. As if my brain can't quite catch up. Throw in the almost-botched B and E and my mother's fixation with a former, possibly-shady FBI agent and I'm a hot-ass mess.

By the time we arrived home, my brain wouldn't shut down as I pondered ways to identify who the Evelyn might be.

I tossed in my bed, stringing ideas together. Internet searches. A family history on Marie. Whoever the woman in the painting is, I feel like it has to be someone special. Why else would Marie deviate from lighthouses and landscapes to a lone portrait?

Somewhere around five, I drifted off to sleep, but my eyes popped open at six forty-five. I attempted to convince my psyche it was time to rest, but, well, epic failure for sure. I dragged my weary body from bed and killed time meditating and browsing the internet until Matt showed up.

All in all, this investigation has been quite the adventure. And that's saying something considering my sister and I recently caught a serial killer.

It's just before eleven when I slide into Matt's father's Buick and—thank you, sweet baby Jesus—see two coffee cups in the holders.

"Hey." His blue eyes twinkle and I'm once again reminded of his ability to constantly be on the move.

This isn't the first time I've ridden in Papa Stephens' car. Matt's is a slick vintage Mustang, not exactly low-key when tailing someone. When on the prowl, borrowing his Dad's has become the norm. The black sedan that millions of Americans drive blends beautifully.

"Hey." I settle in and fasten the belt. "You broke out the Buick."

"Yeah. Your Mom'll spot us in mine." He points to the cup on my side. "I got you a green tea."

"I love you, Matt Stephens."

At that, he rolls his eyes. "You sure you want to do this with me? You look beat."

"I am. I'm not built for this. Put me in my studio for endless hours and I'm in heaven. This chaos? Not my style. But this is my mom we're talking about and I don't trust Alfonzo. He's up to something. It better not be him she's meeting."

Matt backs out, his silence confirming my residence in LaLa Land.

After sipping my tea, I wince as the hot brew hits my lips. "Just the way I like it. What's the plan?"

"Charlie said you guys have that friend-finding app on your phones."

Ah, yes. My sister's paranoia, as much as I like to tease her about it, sometimes comes in handy. Particularly when she insists every member of our family be easily trackable in case someone—say a serial killer—kidnaps us.

I set my tea back in the holder and tap my phone, pulling up the app and—voila. Mom's photo appears on the map. "She's on the Beltway. Heading toward D.C."

Matt hits the gas. "That's good and bad."

"Why?"

"Good because we'll blend into traffic. Bad because we'll blend into traffic. Harder to keep up. We'll see."

At this time of morning, we manage to pick up my mom's location without incident.

M Street in Georgetown.

Parked cars line both sides and pedestrians wander the cobblestone sidewalks, their arms filled with goodies they've picked up in the shopping mecca of the area.

I check my phone again. There. A few cars ahead. "I think she's stopped. She may have snagged street parking."

"Okay. Well, not ideal. Looks like we're following on foot. Let's get a visual on her and then figure out what we're doing."

Matt avoids the line of stopped vehicles in front of us by pulling into a no-parking zone in front of a fire hydrant.

The problem with our handy-dandy app is it doesn't give exact addresses. I have a street name, but unless my mother sends me her exact location, we won't know where on this part of the block she actually is. And with the number of stores and restaurants, we'll lose her in seconds.

I hit the lock button on the door. "I'm gonna hop out so we don't miss her."

"Meg, hang on."

I'm sure Matt has a justifiable argument and, God knows, if Charlie were here, she'd accuse me of being too spontaneous. All I know is I want information. Specifically, who my mother is meeting. I don't want to admit my suspicions. As if avoiding the obvious—that she's sneaking around with Al—will make it go away.

"You park," I tell Matt. "I'll follow her."

I shut the door before an argument is launched. In front of me are two moms pushing strollers, behind them a jogger and a woman walking four dogs.

That's talent.

And, whoopsie. Behind that is my mother. Coming straight at me.

Damn.

Probably should've listened to whatever argument Matt had been about to make.

But...too late now.

"Hey!"

I swing back around and...double damn.

A cop has pulled beside the Buick, blocking Matt's exit. His passenger window is rolled down. "You," the cop says to Matt. "You're in front of a hydrant. Move it."

Really? It's bad enough my mom is walking straight toward us and now we have Captain America hassling Matt.

Two storefronts down, mom treks on while Matt assures the officer he's about to move.

Hide.

It's all I can think. If she spots me, this whole operation is ruined. Matt might be able to avoid her given he's driving the Buick, rather than his own car. But me?

My mother is far from stupid. She'll tag us as following her the minute she sees us.

My pulse kicks up and I swing to my right, searching for any available alcove I can duck into. Nothing. The street corner offers me zippo.

No place to hide. Frantically, I scan the area. Nothing.

A stinging sensation rips straight down my neck. Move. Now.

I do the only thing I can and hop back into the car, ducking low.

"Meg," Matt says, his voice a cross between what-the-hell-and you-must-be-crazy. "You're killing me. Do you not see this cop?"

"Get rid of him," I say. "Mom is right there. If she sees me, we're toast."

He peers out the windshield and grunts. "She just went into the deli."

Phew. I scoot back up and let out a breath. "Close one."

Just as I glance at Matt, the cop steps to the driver's side. So much for staying low-key.

"Thanks, Meg," Matt mutters.

"Sorry." I scrunch my nose. "Guess I should've stayed in the car."

"Ya think?"

"License and registration," the cop says.

Matt reaches for the glovebox and digs around, coming up with the latter. "Sorry, officer. I was dropping my friend off."

"I see that." He peers at me through dark sunglasses. "Miss, are you okay?"

His eyes might be hidden but the tight skin of his face indicates he's young. Maybe not even thirty. If he's a rookie, we could be screwed. They tend to play only by the book. No slack.

Ever.

"Yes." I bob my head. "I'm fine."

He purses his lips slightly, then moves his attention to the registration and Matt's license. "This your car?"

"No, sir. It's my father's."

"And, where is he?"

Matt's head dips forward an inch. "At home. I borrowed it."

Now he looks back at me. "Miss, why were you crouching? You hiding from someone?"

Um, yeah.

Except, I can't exactly tell this cop I'm tailing my mom who thinks a serial killer lives across the street.

When I don't answer, Matt shifts from the cop and grits his teeth at me.

"No, officer. Not...hiding."

He finally takes his glasses off and pegs me with laser sharp green eyes. "You know what?"

Uh-oh. I don't like the sound of that.

He takes two steps backward. "Out of the car, please."

Matt lets out a sigh. "Officer—"

"Out. Of. The. Car. Now."

Rookies.

"I'm sorry," I tell Matt.

He holds up a hand. "Just do what he says."

We exit and I try to ignore the rubberneckers as they drive by. The pedestrians don't even bother to keep going. They stop and stare like we're a circus act.

At this point, we might just be.

A second cop pulls up and directs Matt and I to the rear.

"You mind if I search your car?" The first asks.

"Not at all," Matt says. "I'm a PI. You'll see my license in my wallet. Center console."

The cop nods. "Any weapons? Anything that can hurt me?"

"No, sir."

The cop peers through the rear driver side window. "What's this briefcase on the backseat?"

"Work stuff."

The half second it took Matt to answer brings my gaze to him. I know him. Know the cadence of his voice, his vocal cues and how fast he responds when he's confident of the answer.

That minute, piddly pause?

Trouble.

While cop number two stands with us, the rookie opens the door, retrieves the briefcase and sets it on the hood.

What's in there? I look back to Matt, but his chin is up, his eyes forward.

It's one of those square ones with snapping locks I used to see on old televisions shows from the sixties.

Snap-snap. The cop lifts the lid. "Whoa," he says.

Whoa?

"Officer," Matt says, "those are—"

"IDs" The cop holds up what looks like a bunch of credit cards and maybe driver's licenses. "All with different names. Frank Murdoch, Jeff Racine, Mel Watkins."

Of course he has fake IDs. He's a private investigator. Call them tools of the trade when he's working a case.

I dare not say it though because the way this cop has keyed in on them indicates he's not about to let Matt slide on having them.

Not with the rampant identity fraud plaguing citizens.

"Okay, Mr. Stephens. Or Mr. Racine. Or is it Watkins?"

"It's Stephens," Matt says.

The cop tosses the IDs back in the briefcase and snaps it closed again. "I guess we'll see about that. Both of you, hands behind your back. You're coming with me."

After recruiting my sister's boyfriend for help and being cleared by the cops, I'm escorted to the lobby of the police station. Matt must still be inside, leaving me nothing to do but wait. I glance around at the benches along either wall.

As lobbies go, this isn't the worst I've seen, but it could use a fresh coat of paint to liven up the dull white. Given the age of the building—I'm guessing somewhere around a hundred—the marble might be original.

For a few seconds, I stand there studying the veins in the

floor and simply breathe. I'm exhausted, strung out and will no doubt face Charlie's wrath for dragging JJ into this mess.

Banner day.

Voices bring me from my mini-meditation. An officer has just handed the woman behind the glass wall a stack of paperwork.

I nod and she offers me a bland smile.

Oh, the things she must see in a day.

If I'm stuck here, I might as well sit. I set my bag on one of the walnut benches along the wall and drop, resting my head back. A nap would do me some good. Maybe a quick mediation while I wait on Matt.

Before I can close my eyes, I spot the bulletin board on the opposite wall. It's covered with flyers and posters for area events. A car seat safety check, fire department fundraiser, what looks like press releases and the requisite most-wanted posters.

My mind drifts back to Jerome, my love, sitting across from me in the conference room, studying files. Did anything beat a supportive man?

I don't think so. As looney as the Schock family is, Jerome rolls with it. A gift for sure.

Most wanted.

I lift my head, my eye zooming in on one of the posters.

Ohmygod.

I snap to, rifling through my bag for my phone. Come on, come on, where are you?

Something niggles and as I dig, I glance to where the woman behind the wall eyes me.

If she thought I was nuts before, I must look like a flat-out psycho right now. Psycho. Police station.

I force a smile that hopefully conveys my lack of wanting to blow up the building. "I just remembered something," I say. "I need to call my sister."

She nods, but I'm still seeing a boatload of this-chick-might-be-dangerous in her eyes.

Whatever.

My fingers brush something hard—got it. I whip out my phone and hit Charlie's name.

"Where the hell are you?" She asks.

"Police station. I'll explain later. I think I know who Evelyn is."

15

Charlie

"Why are you there?" I ask as I pull out of the Valley View Golf Course. I put the AC on full blast and tug my blouse from my sweating chest. My lunch meeting with Mike Grenado, Al's former partner, was a bust.

"It's Matt's fault," Meg says, and I hear the tone of an inside joke. "You really should've stuck to your guns and fired him last night. Yes, Mom met Al. You were right about that, but I have no idea what they're doing. We got a little...sidetracked."

"Do you need a lawyer?" Adjusting my vents, I take the long drive to leave the golf grounds, passing a few of the diehards ignoring the heat. I merge into traffic, thankful for my Bluetooth. "Are you at the downtown station? I'm on my way."

"I think we're good. There's a little problem with fake IDs but I called JJ and he's on it."

"You did what?"

"I'll explain later. I need you to go to my desk and get my

sketchbook. Inside is a list of criminals. Search for the name Christopher Svenson."

"Who's he?"

"Career criminal on that list we researched. He had a girl-friend he traveled with. I think her name was Evelyn."

"Like the woman on the painting?"

"Yep. Do you see the sketchbook?"

It's a stretch to assume the woman in the portrait is the same one on a most wanted list from twenty-plus years ago. I put on my signal to merge into the traffic and accelerate. "I played phone tag all morning with Al's partner, and he finally left a message to meet him at the Valley View Golf Course pavilion for lunch. He lives on the course apparently, but he never showed. I'm on my way back to the office now."

"Did you go to his house? Ask around if he was out on the greens?"

"Check and check. He wasn't home, or he was avoiding me, and no one's seen him. I think the asshole stood me up."

"Oh, here's Matt. I gotta run. I'll meet you back at the office."

I beat her there, and Haley and I tackle her workspace. Yes, it takes two because my sister is no neat freak. There are art supplies, files, and books everywhere. She has sticky notes all over her laptop, and an assortment of tote bags and clothes slung over various pieces of furniture.

Today, Haley has an interesting combo of pink and purple in her hair, and she's not the brightest thing in the room. My sister loves art of all kinds and there are bold canvases on the walls, along with statues and other pieces from multiple countries amongst the shelves and tops of cabinets.

"Do you know what her sketchbook looks like?" I ask Haley, feeling slightly guilty for not paying more attention when Meg has it out.

Haley shuffles a stack of books aside . "She has, like, three. Do you know which she's referring to?"

In all honestly, she probably has more than that. "The one she's been using this week. Does that help?"

Haley nods. Her unicorn hair falls over her shoulders as she shifts a day calendar to the side. "The green. Here it is."

She hands it to me and I see it's stuffed with papers. "Thanks. I'd be lost without you."

The phone rings in the outer room and she searches a moment for Meg's desk phone, but doesn't find it, and takes off at a run. I flip through the book, hearing her answer the call at her own desk.

The usual drawings of nature, an age progression of herself, and...wait, what's this?

Jerome.

She's done a series of portraits. His left side, front, right, the back of his head, neck, and shoulders. She's caught him looking down, laughing, staring into space.

So damn good. While her office looks like a bomb went off in it, the sketches are neat, clear, precise. Like the woman herself, her art is unique. Jerome appears as though he might come to life on the page.

I've always envied Meg's gift. I love how vibrant her inner world is, and I'm thankful she's added so much color to my outer one.

I flip until I find the list of names she wrote out by hand, along with their status. Evelyn Jacoby. Girlfriend of Sven, one of the London Fog bank robbers. Aliases: Eve Jacobs; Lyn Jacobs; Lyn Jacobi.

According to Meg's notes, Evelyn's boyfriend, who also had a multitude of aliases, is dead. Jacoby is missing. Last known whereabouts the D.C. area during the bank robbing spree.

I return the sketchbook to the desk and take the list to my office. I call Matt's girlfriend, Taylor, and miracle of miracles, she answers on the third ring. I ask our FBI insider in charge of cold cases if she'll look up who the agents were that investigated the London Fog Gang in the 90s. I want to see if I can interview them and get any background information on Evelyn.

Taylor tells me she's on her way to a meeting and will call me back.

When I'm thinking, I rock in my chair. Back and forth, back and forth. Could this Evelyn and the woman in the painting be the same? Was Marie hanging around a known felon and his girlfriend? Is she herself wanted by police?

Is Gayle?

Surely if either were, it would've come up in our investigation. Al certainly would've checked that possibility out, wouldn't he? This timeframe matches when he was still at the Bureau.

I'm digging in to what I can find myself about Evelyn and what ties she might have to Marie and Gayle, when my contact at Family Ties interrupts. "Preliminary results will be ready at three," Chuck says. "You can pick them up then."

"Are you kidding?" It's already two-thirty. "Did you put a rush on them?"

Chuck doesn't sound happy about it. "When the AG asks for something to be done fast, we aim to please. Lucky for you, the original medical examiner had the DNA extracted from both the teeth and femur bones when the body was found in 2004. Our forensic expert ran separate samples, and will have a complete new analysis done in a few hours, but even with our advances in technology, it'll probably show the same results." He clears his throat. "Remember this the next time I need your services. I expect a deep discount."

"Your ex giving you problems again?" I tease. I've yanked his chain several times in the past few months, but he owes me after the dirt I found on that woman. "Look, I really appreciate it, and I'll put a good word in with the AG for you."

I hang up to find Haley walking in with a pink message slip. "Mike Grenado." She hands it to me. "Still playing phone tag?"

I sigh, reading the message. "He stood me up after I drove all the way out to Valley View. Lives on the ninth hole. I suppose meeting with a PI asking questions about his former partner slipped his mind."

"That must be why he said he's sorry." She stares at the painting JJ bought me. A far cry from the masterpieces Meg has. "He must have the bucks if he lives on that golf course."

"Must have."

On the slip, in her curly handwriting, she has in quotes, *Sorry about today. Al – good guy, great partner.*

I glance up at her. "That's all he said?"

She nods and we hear the beep of the front door. Mom's voice echoes down the hall before Haley gets two steps into the hall. "Charlie? Meg? Anyone here?"

Haley intercepts her and they exchange a greeting. Mom appears in the doorway and I stare at her in surprise. "Lunch over already?"

"Well, it *is* nearly three. My car quit, can you believe it? I tried calling your sister to come get me, but she's not answering. Where is she?"

Meg being at the police station after she and Matt were tailing Mom and Al is a subject I don't want to get in to. "I'm not sure," I lie. "Why didn't you call me?"

"I knew you were busy."

She didn't call me because her date was with Al. "It was nice your friend could drop you off. Doesn't she want to come in?"

Mom glances away, brushing her hands over her linen pants. "Oh no. She had to get going."

Sure she did. "Any clue as to what's wrong with the car?"

"The starter's acting up. My, uh, friend called a service and had it towed to the garage."

"Mom, I know you had lunch with Al. You don't have to hide it."

She seems shocked. "How did…"

"Private investigator, remember? Former FBI profiler? Forensic psychologist?"

A shake of her head, topped off with an eye roll. "Okay, fine. You got me. We were discussing the case, that's all."

I close my laptop and stand, grabbing my bag. No word from Taylor, I have a file of facts to read about Evelyn later, and Meg's hasn't shown up yet. "How about you come with me to pick up the lab results on our unidentified body?"

This lights up my mother's face. "They're in already? That was fast."

"Fortune smiles on us occasionally." Fortune, aka JJ.

We say goodbye to Haley. Mom follows me out the front door, right on my heels, talking away about the unidentified woman and what she hopes we'll discover about her family. How this might bring them some peace. I refrain from mentioning that if the DNA didn't turn up any connections before, it might not now, either.

The heat is less intense today, but the humidity is just as bad. Mom is still talking as we climb into my car and I back out, heading for the main road. Some days, investigating is playing phone tag. Others it's going back and forth, trying to find witnesses, or surveilling people to get pictures. Witnesses stand you up. Your sister ends up at the police station. I can't wait to hear the story behind that.

On a rare occasion, something easy and helpful happens, like DNA results being ready in record time. I take those gifts with pleasure.

Mom is chatting away about two of the women in the group with her, and I'm thinking about Evelyn, when my driver's side window explodes.

A scream rips through the air. I wrench the wheel.

Glass sprays over me, smacks my face, catches in my hair. A bullet lodges in my dash.

A fiery sharp sting on my left arm, and the stickiness of warm blood.

Bam.

A second bullet hits the front tire.

Mom screams again as the front end jerks. We skid.

As I try not to lose control, car horns blare behind us. The rear end swings around, my ears ringing from the exploding glass and my mother's cries.

Get off the road. Now.

Gripping the wheel with all I've got, I try not to hit anyone and still move away from the shooter, wherever he or she might be. Another car? Somewhere off to the side?

The car won't cooperate.

I stop the fishtail and the wheels hit something slick—oil on the road—and spin the opposite way. I'm pumping the brakes as hard as I can, but I can't keep us from flying down the embankment and up the other side.

The brakes refuse to work, but the telephone pole we hit head-on stops us cold.

16

Meg

I'm standing at the gate of the impound lot waiting for Matt to retrieve the Buick. The car is sitting in front of the small office so I'm assuming he's handling paperwork.

My phone rings and JJ's name lights up the display. I owe him big for handling this. A bottle of expensive scotch might be a nice gesture. It strikes me as something he'd like.

I accept and lift the phone to my ear. "Mr. U.S. Attorney, thank you very much for the help."

"Meg," he says, voiced rushed and immediately setting me on edge. "Where are you?"

"The impound lot. We're getting the car back. What happened?"

"I just got a call. It's Charlie. And your mom. Car accident."

For a second, I can't move. It's as if my body has gone numb. A futile attempt to absorb the shock. I don't have time for this though.

Charlie.

Mom.

Accident.

Then I'm moving, my feet pounding the gravel, heading toward that damned office. "I just talked to her."

"I'm on my way to the scene. I don't have details yet. They're alive. I'll text the address."

My relief comes hard and fast. A literal gut punch that halts me midway. I bend over, suck hot, stagnant air in and force myself to breathe.

They need me. I'm not allowed to freak out right now.

"Meg?" JJ asks. "Are you okay?"

"I'm fine. Just...get to them. We're right behind you."

I punch off and start hollering. "Matt! Matt!"

The office door opens and he sticks his head out. "Where's the fire?"

"No fire. Charlie and Mom were in an accident."

He angles away, speaking to someone inside then bolts to the Buick, firing it up just as I reach him.

Before we clear the gate, JJ's text comes in and we race to Charlie's location.

We barrel around the corner and Matt slams on the brakes before he plows into the stopped vehicles trying to merge into the left lane.

My gaze zooms in on the swirling red lights of an ambulance and, to the right of that, the front end of my sister's car mashed against a telephone pole.

"Oh, my God."

A jackhammer unleashes itself in my chest sending stabs of pain in all directions.

I jerk on the handle and shove the door open.

"Meg, wait."

No. Charlie and my mother were in there. I charge toward a

cop, standing guard. He holds his hands up. "Sorry. Restricted area."

My ass.

"That's my sister's car."

I keep my pace and the cop, a beefy guy who looks near retirement, shifts to his right to intercept me, but—whoopsie—I juke the other way, hopping just out of reach and blow by him.

"Hey!" He yells.

Ahead of me two more uniformed cops and a tall man in a navy suit—JJ—angles back.

"Stop her!" The cop shouts.

JJ rushes forward, his mouth moving fast and they stand down. JJ walks toward me, arms extended. "Stop. Before you get your butt tased."

My breath comes in short bursts, a product of my panic upon seeing the mess that's Charlie's vehicle.

I halt and wave a hand to the cops while buckets of sweat roll down my back. "How...are...they?"

Dammit. I can't get any air.

"Whoa," JJ says. "Slow down. Concentrate on breathing."

No doubt Charlie has shared my history of panic attacks with him.

"I need you to focus, Meg."

I'm no good to Charlie or Mom this way. I count to three and draw air through my nose, then slowly blow it out my lips.

"Again," he urges.

After the third repetition, my chest no longer feels as if it's about to fracture.

"I'm good," I assure him. "How are they? Please, JJ, tell me they're still alive."

The idea of losing them? I...can't. What would Dad and I do? I shake the thought away. Seatbelts. They always wear them. I hang on to that thought.

"God, Meg, of course they are. I wouldn't..."

He raises one hand and presses his fingers against his forehead hard enough to turn his skin red and it hits me. Big, strong JJ, our go-to guy, was as scared as I was.

I reach for him, squeezing his arm. "We're okay."

He drops his hand, pushes his shoulders back and gives me a curt nod. "We're okay," he repeats. "Your mom is in the ambulance. Head laceration. She must've whacked it on the passenger window."

He's not saying anything about Charlie. They're alive though. He said *that*.

"Where's Charlie?"

"On her way to the hospital." Before I have a chance to speak, he holds his hands up again. "She's conscious and spitting mad."

Thank you. "Of course she is. She loves that car." I peer at the wreckage, the crumpled front end and the blown airbags. "What the hell happened? Did someone cut them off?"

He waves me to follow him and we march by the two cops. At the rear of the ambulance, I pause and peek around the open door.

Mom is perched on a gurney while an EMT checks out a cut on her head.

"Mom?"

She snaps her gaze to me and I can't help it. I jump in and wrap my arms around her. I'm so damned happy to see her.

"I'm all right," she says. "How's Charlie?"

She's the one injured, yet I'm being comforted. I suppose, no matter how old we get, a mother's instinct is to protect.

"JJ said they took her to the hospital, but she's awake and steaming."

She touches my hair, runs her hand down it. "That's good. If she's mad, she's coherent."

"Meg," JJ calls, "I need to steal you for a sec."

I look at the EMT. What I want from him, I'm not sure, but he seems to understand.

He jerks his chin toward the doors. "Go. I'll finish here and you can ride with her. She'll probably need a few stitches."

I squeeze her hand. "I'll be right outside. You're not alone. I promise."

"I know, my girl. Thank you. We need to find Charlie."

I hop off the step. "As soon as we get to the hospital, we will."

"Contact your father."

"I already did. He's on his way back from fishing. I'll call again. Tell him to meet us at the hospital."

JJ grabs my elbow, ushering me to Charlie's mangled car. His long legs outpace my shorter ones so I double-time it to keep up.

"How did this happen?"

My sister is good behind the wheel. Being the security conscious—i.e. paranoid—sort, she's put herself through defensive driving classes and could probably outmaneuver a Hollywood stuntman.

"They were heading to the lab to pick up DNA results."

As we get closer, guys in blue polo shirts and khaki pants walk around the vehicle.

One pauses at the driver's side door and stares at the window—or lack thereof.

The windshield, from my vantage point, is intact. This was a front end collision. How does the side get blown out and not the windshield.

I stop walking and point.

"Why the hell is there no window?" And wait one second. "The tire is flat."

I make a move toward it, but JJ stops me. "You can't."

Watch me. "My mother and sister were in there. You'd better believe I can."

"No, Meg. Seriously. You can't. It's a crime scene."

My head lops forward, the weight straining my neck. What is he *talking* about?

I shake my head. Maybe the stress is frying my brain. "I don't understand. This was an accident, right?"

Please let him tell me it was.

JJ faces me. His arms are at his sides but the fingers of his right hand twitch. Whatever happened, it has him rattled.

And that, I haven't seen very often.

"Someone took a shot at them."

What did that mean exactly? "As in a *gunshot*?"

"Yes."

The word, three simple letters, assaults me. The ground shifts and I take a step back as my blood pressure plummets.

"Whoa." JJ grabs my arm and I force myself to concentrate on the gesture. On him keeping me from losing my balance. On his steady gaze.

Anything to stay upright. My mother and sister need me and I refuse to let shock rule my reaction to this news.

I glance at the ambulance. A laceration. That's what JJ said about mom. If she had a gunshot wound, they'd be on their way to the hospital already.

"Charlie," I say. "She was hit."

It comes out a statement. Somehow, I know it's true. I feel it.

JJ wastes no time in nodding. "In the arm. She had her hand on the wheel." He holds his left out to demonstrate. "She got hit here." He points to his forearm. "The bullet went straight through and landed in the dashboard."

"One shot?"

"Two, actually. The second hit the tire. Whoever it is, is a terrible shot."

"Ma'am?"

I turn and spot the EMT standing at the rear of the ambulance. "Time to leave."

With JJ in tow, I make my way to it. "I'm going with Mom. I'll check on Charlie as soon as we get there. Will you keep me informed about what's happening here?"

"Absolutely. And Meg?"

"Yes?"

"Tell her I love her."

I reach the ambulance, hop inside then swing to JJ. "You tell her. She'd rather hear it from you anyway."

For the first time since I arrived on scene, JJ smiles. "You're right. And thank you."

17

Charlie

$\mathcal{M}$y head pounds, throbbing like a damn bass drum inside my skull.

My nose stings from the airbag impact, the powder from it lodging in my chest. I feel like I have asthma, my breathing tight and irregular even after the EMT gives me oxygen.

At the hospital, a nurse named Yolanda says I'm lucky—I only have three tiny pieces of glass in my cheekbone to remove before the doctor stitches me up. Yes, I'll probably have two black eyes tomorrow, thanks to the airbag, and my arm feels like a hundred-pound weight from the bandages the EMT wrapped it in, but, she says, trying to cheer me up, "You're alive!"

She's obviously a glass-half-full type of person.

"How is my mother?" I flinch as she tweezes at one of the slivers.

I hate hospitals, especially emergency rooms. We're behind

MISTY EVANS & ADRIENNE GIORDANO

a curtain, acting as a makeshift wall, as others come and go from the admission desk down the hall. Next to my six-by-nine space, a guy groans on the other side.

The smell of alcohol makes my eyes tear as she dabs at the blood running down my cheek. She's dressed in a SpongeBob scrub top, which seems completely incongruent with the environment. "I believe the second ambulance just arrived with her," she says.

"I need to see her." Paper crinkles as I start to slide off the exam table.

Yolanda is short, has chocolate brown eyes that exude patience and a no-nonsense attitude, and is strong as an ox. Her gloved hand grips my good arm and halts me in my tracks. "Not until we have you stitched up and the doctor has a look at your wounds."

My phone rings from the front pocket of my briefcase across the room on a crowded countertop. I was in a small amount of shock at the scene, but I made sure the EMTs understood I couldn't leave it behind. "I need to get that. It could be my sister."

The dark eyes study me, her smile that of a kindergarten teacher reaching to new depths of patience. She doesn't release me. "Do you want scars on this pretty cheekbone of yours?"

I sense a threat under that smile. "Sorry?"

"You have beautiful skin. Removing glass from it is a delicate procedure." She emphasizes the last two words. "I suggest you sit still and let that ring until I'm done."

"But—"

"Ms. Schock, do you have a clue who runs this ER?"

I bite back a sarcastic reply. She's trying to help and has the right to ask for cooperation.

I flick dust from my dress pants for the umpteenth time, disgusted that they, like my car, are ruined. "You?"

The smile grows, as if she's given me a gold star for getting the answer correct. The strong lamp she's pulled over to help her see spotlights a section of her dark skin. "You're not allowed to use a cell in my ER while being examined. That means ignoring it and sitting absolutely still. If you don't? Your phone will accidentally end up in that waste bin over there. You don't want that, do you?"

The red biohazard symbol mocks me, as if taking Yolanda's side. I shake my head like a good little student, but internally I'm fuming.

She must see it in my eyes and decides to emphasize her point. "Also? I might have to call Dr. Gomez instead of Dr. Marx who is much better with a needle. Her stitches are so precise. Gomez?" She makes a face. "His are dicey." The smile returns. "Do I make myself clear?"

I've possibly met my match here, yet I sense her threats are borderline serious and I'm not in the mood to go more rounds with anyone today. "Crystal."

"Thank you. May I resume my work?"

My phone falls silent. Gritting my teeth so I don't ask her to hurry, I nod and listen hard to the activity on the other side of the curtain.

The usual noise of an ER meets my ears. Phones ringing, people shouting, gurney wheels squeaking. Dr. Gomez is paged. Someone in the hall at the waiting station cries softly. The curtain stops about two feet from the floor, and dozens of different shoes pass by.

My brain circles the accident—the exploding glass, the tire. My mother's screams.

Those will haunt me for a long time.

As Yolanda teases out another piece, and I bite my cheek so as not to swear a blue streak, I think I hear Meg's voice. A flood of relief washes through me and I focus on the floor under the curtain, watching for familiar shoes to come into view. "Meg?" I call, and Yolanda makes a disapproving noise in her throat.

Sure enough, a moment later, blue sneakers with brightly painted daisies appear. My sister shoves the curtain out of the way and shuts her eyes briefly, as if feeling the same relief as I do. "Oh, thank God." She rears back and hollers down the hall. "Found her!"

Yolanda has no option but to stand back as Meg throws her arms around my neck. "JJ said you were all right, but I needed to see it for myself."

Matt jogs in and Yolanda huffs. "Close that curtain, young man," she orders. "You two really should wait in the hall until the doctor has seen my patient."

Meg gives her a *bite me* look, then scans my face. "You are okay, right?"

My phone starts again. I glance at Yolanda, who arches a brow as if to say *try me*.

Matt reaches over and tugs on my sleeve. "You gave us a good scare. How's the arm?"

Before I can answer, Yolanda points her tweezers at him. "We won't know until the doctor looks at it, which she won't do until I have the glass out of this cheek and she can stitch her up, so what do you think the wise move would be right now for you all?"

She smiles—all patience and half-full-glass of goodness—and they both blink. They also step away in unison after I give them a nod.

"Passive-aggressive much?" Megs mutters under her breath, shooting Yolanda an innocent smile.

"What about Mom?" I ask, attempting to defuse the situation. "Is she okay? Her head was bleeding." I rub my own, Yolanda lightly slapping my hand. "Things are a little blurry still."

"She's fine," Meg replies. "Shook up, and needs stitches as well for a cut on her head, but otherwise fine. Dad should be here soon."

"Tell us what happened," Matt says. "Did you get a look at the shooter?"

Yolanda scores a direct hit and I suck in a breath. "Two down," she croons. "You're doing great."

The kindergarten teacher is back.

Meg shifts to stand next to me and squeezes my hand. I return it. "I didn't. What do the cops think? Any witnesses?"

Matt shakes his head. "The one I spoke with at the scene suggested you cut someone off and they went road rage on you."

I scrunch up my face then un-scrunch it when my sore nose balks. "I didn't. Mom and I had merged onto East Madena, heading for Family Ties. There wasn't even that much traffic. Maybe the shooter meant those bullets for someone else?"

He rubs his chin, contemplating this theory. "I can see the first being an error, but two? Is it possible one of your current cases has upset someone?"

"Owww!" I say as Yolanda tugs the last shard out. She places it in a container, drops her tweezers into a sterilizing jar, and dabs at my cheek with another antiseptic wipe. The sucker burns and I bite my lower lip, refusing to jerk away.

"There now." She pats my leg. "All done. I'll get Dr. Gomez."

"You said if I cooperated, you'd get Dr. Marx."

She swings the light away and flips the switch. Her gloves are removed with two loud snaps, and she drops them in the waste bin. "Oh, I'm sorry, I forgot. She's off today."

With a cheeky smile, she sweeps past Meg and Matt, whips the curtain aside and disappears.

"She's a character," Meg says, laughing quietly. "I think I like her. Is this Gomez guy bad news? Do you want us to take you across town to a different acute care?"

I push off the exam table, crinkling paper in my wake, and head for my briefcase. "I just want out of here, period."

"You need to have your wounds checked," Meg argues.

I snatch my phone and see I've missed a call from Al. *Hmm.* Mom must've texted him, but why isn't he calling her instead of me? Maybe she isn't answering either.

An older woman sticks her head in. "Miss Schock?"

I assume this is Dr. Marx and Yolanda is laughing her ass off at me somewhere down the corridor. I wave the woman in, but keep my phone. "That's me."

She and another woman step inside the makeshift room, flashing badges. "I'm Detective Young." She's Hispanic and short, like my nurse. "This is my partner, Detective Ansel."

Ansel is taller, with silvery blond hair and lots of wrinkles.

I set the phone on my briefcase and shake their hands. Young takes out a blue notebook and flips it open. "What can you tell us about the shooting?"

I recite the facts. The memory of my smashed-up car flashes in front of me, Mom's screams a distant echo. I swallow the white-hot anger pushing up into my throat. "Have you spoken to any witnesses?"

The two exchange a brief glance. Young flips to a blank page. "I understand you're a private investigator. Can you think of anyone who might want to harm you?"

"Or your mother?" Ansel adds.

Someone who'd want to hurt Mom? Meg and I lock eyes, my gut turning somersaults. Gayle? Marie? Is it possible they figured out we broke into their house and they're pissed?

People have been shot for less.

My phone rings again. It's JJ. "Sorry." I hold up a finger. "I need to take this."

"Charlie." Meg's voice is chastising. "Can't it wait?"

"How about hate mail?" Detective Ansel asks, as if she didn't hear either of us.

I give her a questioning look.

"From you being in the spotlight," Young explains. "You've been on the news a lot recently, haven't you?"

Okay, Cagney and Lacey. My phone continues to ring. "Mad Dog, fill them in," I tell him, turning my back on all of them and punching the answer button.

"Hey," JJ says, and I unclench my jaw. "Are you out of the ER already?"

"Still here. Waiting for the doc." Behind me, Matt starts listing the various cases on our docket. "Is my baby totaled?"

"You were shot and that's your first question?"

"Actually, my first question was about Mom, but I'm told she's okay." I'm angry as hell, but if I start down that road with him or the detectives, I might explode. "I'm fine, my car is not."

He knows she was a gift to myself the day I left the FBI and started Schock Investigations with Meg. I saved for years to buy her, and even though she's nearing a hundred thousand miles, I wouldn't trade her for anything.

The detectives are now quizzing Meg about the media publicity we've received over the last few cases.

"I could use some good news," I say to JJ on a deep exhale. "Tell me she's fixable."

"She's fixable," he lies. "I'm on my way there. Do you need anything? I can stop by your place and pick up an overnight bag for you."

"I'm not staying in the hospital. The bullet went straight through, so once the wound is cleaned and my cheek is stitched, I'm out of here."

"Unless the doctor says otherwise."

My anger overrides my good sense. "I'm fine. Honestly. I need to figure out who shot at us and hand their ass to them. Protect my mother until I do. Besides, I've had worse injuries."

"You've never been shot!"

JJ has. His was much, much, more serious, and it was my fault. I nearly lost him because of my stupidity.

"Sorry, I know it sounds like I'm not taking this seriously, but I am."

"If that bullet had been even a few inches off..."

"I'm aware." Yolanda and her doctor would be digging it out of my brain.

My days in the Bureau were spent mostly behind a desk, analyzing criminals. I'm a trained agent, able to use a variety of weapons and I practice every week so I don't lose my skills, but I never drew my gun during my tenure. I was never shot at.

"It's been on my bucket list." I try to lighten the tension. "I can check it off now."

JJ curses under his breath, not appreciating my attempt at humor.

From behind me, Meg calls my name. "Charlize Lauren Schock. Get off the phone. Your doctor is here."

I turn to find a woman—Dr. Marx by her name tag—squeezing into the already stuffed room. *Damn you, Yolanda.*

But I gotta give the nurse points for making me squirm.

The doctor glances at me, then the detectives, her full mouth turning down. She's taller than all of us and I wonder if her large hands really are as precise as Yolanda claims. "Ms. Schock, would you kindly get back on the exam table?" Her steely gaze shifts to Young and Ansel. "You two wait outside."

"We have more questions," Young says.

Yolanda busts in. She waves at the women to vamoose, even as she works that smile of hers. "You'll have to save them until later. This is an emergency room and our patient needs medical care. She's in shock, can't you see that? Do you have no compassion? This woman was shot and her poor momma injured. I'll call you when she's ready to talk."

"But—" Ansel tries, although she does look a little chagrined at the bawling out.

"I'm not in shock," I argue, but I wink at Yolanda.

"Charlie?" JJ's voice comes from the phone.

As Yolanda nearly shoves the two detectives out, I go back to him. "There is one thing I need you to do for me. Go to Family

Ties and pick up the DNA results for our unidentified female. Chuck's going to put them into the ancestry database and see if we get any hits there, but I want Meg to upload them to GenCo."

Before he can answer, I cover the receiver, another thing on my list for today popping into my head. "Matt, see if Taylor can find a picture of Evelyn Jacoby. The Bureau surely investigated her in the '90s because of her boyfriend."

"Miss Schock," the doctor says sternly, pointing at the table.

At the same time, Yolanda tries to remove Meg and Matt. My sister stands her ground, going eye-to-eye with the feisty nurse. "Charlie, do you want us to leave?"

"Charlie?" JJ's worried voice.

"Yeah, I'm here," I tell him, hopping up and presenting my face. "I want them to stay," I tell Yolanda.

"Put the phone down," Dr. Marx says.

"I've been thinking it over," I say to all of them in general, holding up a couple of fingers at her to beg for two seconds. "If this wasn't some random road rage shooting, we've rattled someone's cage. And, crazy as it sounds, given Mom was in the car with me, it might have something to do with us digging around about Gayle."

Yolanda grabs the phone from my hand. "I warned you."

"Hey," I say, indignant.

She clicks the end button, walks the two steps across the tiny room, and gives me a big smile as she dangles it over the waste bin.

18

Meg

*W*hile my sister and mom are tended to, I take Matt into the hallway. Two of the people I love most just survived a murder attempt.

And I'm pissed.

Whoever it was, I want their head on a stake.

Right.

Now.

I drag Matt to a quiet corner—if there is such a thing—of the ER. "I hate to ask—"

"Say it. I love them, too. Whatever we have to do, we'll do."

His crystal blue eyes possess a fierce determination that makes me thankful we have such a good friend. Total team player ready to protect us.

"Thank you," I reply. "You'll always have a place in our family. I hope you know that."

From now on, I'll tell him more often. He truly is the brother we never had.

"I know. Now what do you need?"

"Can you ask Taylor to pull whatever she has on this Chris Svenson guy? Maybe there's something in his file regarding Evelyn Jacoby. It's no coincidence Marie's work is titled *Evelyn*. I'd also like a photo of her. We'll see if the painting is even a close resemblance."

He's already pulling out his cell. "Of course. We can check online for photos."

"I did that. The ones that came up weren't a match or the dates were wrong."

Matt holds up his phone. "Give me a couple minutes."

"Thank you."

Without warning the day's events sneak up on me. My head begins to throb and the stiffness in my neck might be the cause. So damned tired.

"Meg?"

I draw a breath and meet his gaze. Then his arms are around me, wrapping me up tight and I'm so damned grateful tears flood my eyes.

"They could've died."

My voice is rough, battered by my messy emotions.

"But they didn't," he murmurs. "They're fine and we'll find whoever caused this. Okay?" He backs away and meets my eye, making sure he has my complete focus. "Trust me. We will."

I nod, happily taking refuge in his confidence. My world, despite the day, isn't shattered.

I settle into the thought, let my body absorb the fact. A sense of calm neutralizes my headache and I grip his arms. "Thank you. For everything."

"You're welcome."

"Meg!"

At the sound of my father's panicked voice, I spin away from

Matt. Dad is charging toward me in his cargo pants and lucky fishing T-shirt. He must've broken speed records.

I rush to him, my arms extended. "They're fine," I say as he crashes into me, nearly crushing me with his hug. "They're both good," I whisper, knowing full well what he's feeling right now. "We're okay. I promise you, we all are."

Twenty minutes later, after leaving him in charge of Mom and Charlie, Matt and I hop into the Buick. I hate leaving my family, but Charlie has made the case that JJ is on his way and it was more important that we figure out who tried to commit murder.

Can't say I disagree.

We walk into a coffee shop two blocks from the Hoover building and join Taylor who is sitting toward the back. Given the late afternoon hour, the place is quiet with only one other table occupied.

Taylor stands as we approach. As usual, she's dressed in a classy black suit, the pants fitted enough to be sexy but professional. Taylor has that ability about her. All business, yet feminine in a truly powerful way.

We exchange the requisite hellos and she inquires about Mom and Charlie. After giving her a ten-second report, she indicates the chairs, then reclaims her seat. "I can't give you anything," she says.

Dammit.

My energy plummets. Between my mother and sister involved in a shooting and Taylor's inability to help, this has been a fucker of a day. Still, she wouldn't have dragged us down here if she couldn't help so I hang on to a bit of hope.

"As in physical documents," she clarifies. "Off the record, I can tell you what I know."

Hope. Always a good thing.

I nod. "That works."

"I'll say this," she continues, "it's a good thing Chris Svenson is dead because he was a bad dude."

"Seriously?" Matt says. "All we found was the bank robbing charge."

"That was the least of it. He was also violent. Not during the robberies, but based on what I saw in his file, I'm sure eventually it would've gotten to that."

Fascinated, I lean in. "What kind?"

"He had fetishes. Liked his sex rough. Got turned on by a woman choking him during it and assumed it worked for everyone."

Holy cow. I'm not sure what I expected her to say, but that wasn't it. "He was kinky. What does that have to do with Evelyn Jacoby? Maybe she was into it, too."

Taylor shrugs. "Maybe. I didn't see anything on that. He was arrested once. Assault charge. A woman he'd picked up accused him of choking her out during sex."

"Did he rape her?"

"No. The sex was consensual, the choking not so much."

In my research of him, I only went as far as the most wanted poster so this is new.

"Was he convicted?"

"No."

"Charges were dropped, I bet." This from Matt who shakes his head.

Taylor nods. "And the woman fell off the radar. The D.A. at the time decided not to pursue it. He had bigger fish to fry."

"Was this before Svenson dated Evelyn?"

I'm not sure why it matters, but something—no idea what — is niggling at me.

"I believe so. We don't have a lot on her. According to the file, the money from the previous bank robberies was never recovered. Svenson and the other members of the London Fog Gang died during a takedown."

All of this is good information, but Evelyn and her connection to Gayle and Marie is why we're here. "What about Evelyn? Did she have a criminal record? Was she part of the gang?"

"Not that I could see. She had to have known he was a criminal, though. They were living together at the time. When agents searched the apartment her stuff was gone."

"She ran?"

"It appears so. And the money from the previous robberies was never found. The Bureau believes she took the money."

Matt meets my eye. "She could be living under a new identity somewhere."

"Could be." Taylor pulls her phone from her purse. "Matt said you saw a painting of a woman named Evelyn?"

Not knowing how much Matt shared about our B and E, I simply nod.

Taylor taps at her screen, then holds it so I can see a photo of a young woman with muddy brown hair. "Is this her?"

19

Charlie

*M*y parents drive me to the office against their wishes.

Mom keeps insisting I go home with them so she could take care of me. Because of the stress of all of this, a lot of crazy emotions have surfaced. I teared up at the hospital when she made the offer, but then realized there was nothing she could do to help me feel better. The only thing that's going to do that is if I catch the shooter.

And kick his ass.

Yolanda didn't drop my phone in the waste bin, thank goodness, but she did keep it until the doctor was done with me. While I wiped it off with an alcohol pad as we pulled away from the hospital, I made sure Dad was ultra-aware of anyone who might follow or be waiting at their home. My gut says Mom's not the target, but if whoever did this wants to get to me, my family is the way to do it.

During the drive, I call Justice Greystone and request security for my parents. He's sending his bruiser of a former Secret Service agent, Tony, to keep an eye on them.

Meg and Matt are now with Taylor downtown, and Meg texted that they have news regarding Evelyn and her identity. She shared a few details, but I had to read it three times before any of it sank in. The point that stands out to me is Evelyn Jacoby could be our missing link to figuring this damn case out in more ways than one.

Haley channels my mother as soon as I step in the front door. She walks me to my office, offers to get me coffee. My stomach is a mess, so she brings me a cup of Meg's chamomile tea instead. She asks what else she can do for me, and for a long moment, I'm at a loss for words.

Focus on the shooter. Means, motive, opportunity.

I thank Haley and send her back to her desk. Under my tough veneer, I secretly wonder why I didn't fill the prescription the doctor offered. My cheek throbs and I gently probe the stitches. Damn, that hurts.

My attention is definitely wandering, the physical aches and pains from the crash creeping into every joint. A touch of whiplash is setting up in my neck, making it tight.

Unfortunately, pain medicine and I don't get along. It would only make my head fuzzier, and right now, that's the last thing I need.

As if she reads my mind, Haley appears with an ice pack from our modest kitchen cubby. "It was keeping my lunch chilled."

"You're a lifesaver. Give yourself a raise."

Her smile does me good. "Putting it on my agenda right now."

JJ texts to tell me he has the DNA analysis and is on his way to the hospital. I reply, rerouting him to SI, and a moment later he launches into a lecture about my health and being a workaholic. I hold the ice pack against the back of my neck and close my eyes. He's right, but there's too much swirling in my head to rest.

For several long moments, I focus only on breathing. It works for Meg when she has a panic attack. Unfortunately, my mind refuses to cooperate, and I know the only way to clear it is to write it all down. Standing, I snag the mug of tea, even though I hate the taste, and roll my shoulders before heading to the conference room.

On the way, I stick Haley's ice pack in our freezer. I may need it for my cheek in a while.

My legs feel like Jell-O and my hands shake as I stand in front of the whiteboard. I can barely get the cap off one of the markers, and heated embarrassment—even though I'm alone —rushes into my face when I nearly topple over from the effort. I take more deep breaths and lean on the table, forcing my brain to slow and my body to ignore the lightheadedness coursing through it.

After thirty seconds or so, I get a second wind. I'm grateful when my legs hold steady and the dizziness doesn't rush back as I step to the board.

Who is the shooter? I write it at the top left corner, draw a line under it, and start making notes in three columns.

Means. Motive. Opportunity. I separate each into its own section.

I start with the obvious: Alfonzo Baez – means (certainly knows how to handle a gun). Opportunity (dropped Mom off only minutes before, so he was in the area). Motive (figured out I'm investigating his time with the Bureau? Is that strong enough reason to shoot me?)

Gayle Morton – means (can he shoot a rifle and successfully hit a moving target?) Motive (from the break-in? Seems an extreme reaction unless he's truly a criminal who's realized

MISTY EVANS & ADRIENNE GIORDANO

we're on to him). Opportunity (need to find out where he was at time of shooting).

I add the last one: Unknown Suspect tied to other case. I mentally review the different investigations I'm working, but don't find any solid leads.

In fact, all of these suspects are weak, yet my fuzzy brain keeps niggling at me. I don't believe for a moment the shooting is tied to one of my other cases—no one involved fits the profile of a killer. Maybe that's wishful thinking, and the psychologist inside reminds me I haven't dug deeply enough into the suspects in those embezzlement and fraudulent medical claims cases. Either could be more than they appear on paper.

But the shooter was someone who knew how to use a rifle, knew where I was today.

My gaze goes back to Al's name.

Haley slips in with a yellow notepad and pen. Taking a seat, she watches me carefully, making notes. I can't tell if she's concerned about my health, or has some interest in helping solve the case. Most likely JJ called and told her not to let me out of her sight.

Drawing a long line down the center, I move to the opposite corner and write: *Is the shooting tied to Mom's case? If so, how?*

I stare at that question, sipping the tea. There are too many random people and facts involved with her investigation.

Setting the mug down, I straighten and begin listing all of them, not trying to make any sense of it yet.

Serial killer
Three bodies in Virginia woods
London Fog bank robbers
Lighthouses
Gayle Morton
Evelyn Jacoby
Christopher Svenson

A fresh wave of lightheadedness washes over me and I back up, plunking my butt on the hard conference table again.

"You okay there, Charlie?" Haley asks.

I rub my neck and nod. "You don't usually come in and take notes when I'm working out details of a case."

"Just thought you might need another set of eyes until Meg gets here."

Yep, she's babysitting me. That's okay. I hate like hell to admit weakness, but maybe I need it at the moment.

My attention is drawn back to Svenson—Sven. What is it about his name that bugs me?

"Svenson is Swedish, isn't it?" I ask out loud, as much to myself as her.

"Could be Danish."

I look at the nickname of the bank robbers. Something from Meg's notes tickles my brain. "The London Fog bank robbers were nicknamed that because they had British accents."

Silence from Haley's corner.

"Svenson was born and raised here in the States." I read it in Meg's notes. "Were his parents immigrants? Could be easy to confuse European accents if you're not familiar with them. Maybe the agents who gave them the nickname mislabeled them."

"Is that important?" she asks hesitantly, as if I might criticize the question.

"Probably not, but I wonder..."

She scribbles on her notepad. "What?"

Leaving the room, I return to my office, grab my phone, and see I've missed several texts. Another lecture from JJ about working, and will I go home with him and let him take care of me tonight? A tiny piece of my heart swells and I nearly tear up again.

The other is from Meg telling me they're stuck in traffic but will be here shortly.

I text Taylor and ask if she can share the names of the agents who worked the London Fog robberies with me. I've requested it once, but she never got back to me. That information shouldn't be classified.

I grab my file on the three women buried in Virginia, the notes Meg shared on the lighthouses and Marie, and the timeline I wrote up condensing Mom's records on Gayle. I lug them all back and plunk them on the table. Haley has refilled my tea, steam rising from the mug.

"What do these two sides of the board have in common?" I ask, turning to point, and then regretting the sudden shift.

"Gayle," she volunteers without pause.

I've never talked to him directly. "I wonder if he has any kind of accent?"

She perks up. "Do you have his number? I can call and act like a telemarketer."

I search through notes until I find it. I rattle the digits off and she writes them down. "Do it," I tell her. "Don't be surprised if a woman answers It's his girlfriend, and she's home a lot during the day."

She leaves, and Meg and Matt arrive. They bring me up to speed on the rest of what Taylor shared, and Meg shows me the picture of Evelyn.

While Marie's portrait was hardly done by a master artist, I see similarities. I state the obvious. "Marie knew her. They were friends, isn't that what she told you?"

Meg sets her bag on the table and sinks into a chair, using a hand to brush hair out of her face. The ends are a frizzy mess, thanks to the heat and humidity. "Which means Marie might have known Sven and the bank robbers."

"She must've." I shove the mug to her. I've had enough.

Between that and the adrenaline in my veins now, my head is clearing. "Evelyn was Sven's longtime girlfriend, right?"

"Yep."

Did Gayle know Marie back then? Is he linked to this gang somehow through her? Is that why he's kept odd hours through the years? Stayed in that cabin in Virginia?

It's no coincidence, but... "Were all the London Fog Gang killed?" I ask Meg.

"Yes."

"So Gayle couldn't be one of them," Matt adds, finishing my thought.

He moves to the whiteboard, feet braced and arms crossed, examining my lists. "We should cross-match the locations of the lighthouses against bank robberies in those areas. See if there's a connection."

Meg sips the tea and sighs as if it's the best thing she's tasted all day. "Taylor said Evelyn disappeared around the time Sven died. The money did, too. What are the odds Marie knows exactly what happened to both?"

I take a seat, liking where this is going. Out front, Haley's on the phone and the alarm buzzes. "Taylor told you Sven had a fetish for strangling women, correct?"

My sister looks as excited as I feel. "Our unidentified woman could be Evelyn."

"We should also cross-reference the identified women with Svenson," I say in agreement. "All three were strangled. Maybe he's our serial killer."

At that moment, JJ arrives, looking like a thunderstorm as he slaps an envelope from Family Ties in front of me. "You should be at home in bed."

There's a part of me that wishes he'd whisk me away, take me to his apartment, and force me to stay in bed—with him— the rest of the day. I could use some sleep, some pain relief.

In his eyes, I see the idea is in his head as well. Truth be told, I'm a little surprised he isn't going caveman on me, slinging me over his shoulder and carting me off.

I give him a genuine smile. "I need to figure out who shot at me, the unidentified woman, and what the hell Gayle and Marie have to do with it. After that, I'm all yours."

He leans on the back of the chair next to me. "You don't need to wrap all of this up today. I give you my word, we'll figure it out, but you need rest."

"Have you heard anything from the detectives yet?"

He checks his watch, an expensive Rolex that catches the overhead light. "It's been less than three hours. You have to give them time to do their job, Charlie."

Matt begins scrutinizing each of the items on the whiteboard out loud, cutting off further scolding from my boyfriend and bringing JJ into our discussion with smooth adeptness.

Thank you, Matt.

JJ reluctantly joins our think tank, taking the chair beside me as Matt draws lines between the characters in different colors to signify relationships. I throw out dates from my timeline that he adds to the hodge-podge.

Haley, bless her heart, brings in a fresh pot of coffee and a set of mugs.

"Did you call Gayle?" I ask.

She nods. "I can't say for sure, but there was the slightest hint of a weird accent when he told me how much he hated telemarketers and that I should go do something profane to myself."

"Was it British?"

"Close, but like I said, I'm not sure."

Meg lifts an eyebrow; Matt taps his thumb against his coffee mug. "Accent?" he asks.

I point to the *London Fog* entry. "Svenson is Swedish, or possibly Danish. Maybe our robbers did have an accent— hence their nickname—but maybe it wasn't British."

Meg flips her hand over. "So what?"

So what is right. "It's just one of those details I notice and it bugs me."

I tap the envelope from Chuck. "We need to get this uploaded to GenCo, Meg. Can you do that? I have a feeling we all know the identity of the remains, but without a definitive match, the best we can do is search for a family member and hope to get more information about our unidentified female."

"I'm on it." She takes the file. "What do we do about Gayle and Marie?"

My neck keeps shooting pain into my head, my cheek feels like it's swelling even more, reaching into my eye socket. JJ's admonishment to go home rings in my ears.

Maybe Tylenol would help, maybe his arms around me even more. "Let's not jump the gun," I say, even though I'm dying to confront them. "Just because Marie painted a woman who looks like our dead bank robber's girlfriend, doesn't mean she or Gayle are actually criminals. No judge will grant a warrant based on that. We'll figure out exactly what their connection to Evelyn is, and if she's our unidentified woman in the woods. Then we'll go from there."

"What about Mom?" Meg looks hesitant. "We should bring her in on all of this, right?"

"Yes. I'll call her." My phone buzzes with a text and I see it's from Taylor. The names of the agents in charge of the London Fog case sends another burst of adrenaline up my spine.

When Matt sees the look on my face, his eyebrows crash together. "What is it?"

I glance at the whiteboard, get up and grab the marker I was using. I add Al's name under my list of *Is the shooting tied to Mom's case? If so, how?*

Turning back to the group, I tell them the news. "Alfonzo Baez was the lead investigator in the London Fog bank robberies."

20

Meg

*B*aez is turning out to be the proverbial penny that keeps turning up. Under the guise of being part of this volunteer cold-case group, he's inserted himself into my mother's life. Is it to catch a serial killer or see what she knows?

I rise, more than ready to find out exactly what he wants with her. "All of this can't be a coincidence. I'll load the report and see if we get a hit. While I'm doing that, you go home and rest so Nurse Ratched over here doesn't blow an artery. No offense, JJ."

"None taken," he says.

"I have a couple calls to make. Then I'll go home."

Beside her, JJ grunts. "Charlie—"

"—I can't go yet. If I do, I'll stew all night. Let me do what I need to first."

Realizing she's dug in, JJ shakes his head. "You've got thirty minutes. Then I'm carrying you out of here if I have to."

Charlie bats her eyelashes at the Emperor. "Oooh, won't that be fun."

They're so twisted and perfect for each other, my heart does a little dance. JJ is the love of my sister's life. I sense it in the way her wistful gaze lingers on him, how she talks about him. In the easy gestures and soft touches she gives him almost constantly. As if she can't stand to break the connection.

"It's a plan. Half an hour then JJ goes caveman. I'll be in my office if you need me."

Ten minutes later, I stare at my laptop screen, disbelief surging and morphing into an adrenaline rush that bolts me from my desk chair.

"Charlie!"

I tear into the hallway, pass the conference room where JJ is on his phone and rush into her office and find her half standing. Her skin is pale and the dark circles under her eyes do nothing to alleviate the overall appearance of exhaustion. She really should be in bed.

"Sit." I point to her chair. "And after I tell you my news, you're going home."

"I'm fine," she snaps, probably pissy I'm ordering her around. Well, too bad. She lowers herself down, bracing her hands on the desk for a gentler landing. "What are you screaming about? You scared the hell out of me."

"I got a hit from GenCo."

Her eyebrows lift a smidge. "On Evelyn?"

The fatigue must be frying Charlie's brain, but I take the stressful day into consideration and refrain from a smartass comment.

But, hello? Of course. Who the hell else would it be? "Yep. It's a match on the paternal side. A male. Looks like a half-brother."

"No way."

"Yes, way. Eric Bronson. He lives in Wilmington, Delaware."

Again she pushes up, attempting to move fast but wincing when her body apparently fights back. "That's only two-and-a-half hours. If we leave now, we'll be there by eight."

My sister. The lunatic. If she even thinks I'm letting her take a road trip she's crazier than I've ever given her credit for.

"*We* aren't doing anything."

Her mouth opens, but I'm ready for her and poke my finger. "Hey. Knock it off. We need you, but you're banged up and exhausted. You're no good to us this way. Go home. Get some rest and be battle-ready tomorrow. I'll grab Matt and go see Evelyn's brother."

In response, I receive her resting bitch face. As if that might terrify me into letting her go.

I let out a snort. "Please. You don't scare me, Charlie Schock."

"I know." She gives in and lowers herself. "This pisses me off. This whole damned day does. This poor woman's remains have been sitting in a morgue when all they had to do was upload the DNA again."

Her outrage is warranted, but she's also been around law enforcement long enough to know its limitations.

She holds up a hand. "I know what you're going to say. It's a budgeting thing. The state doesn't have the money to investigate every cold case, blah, blah, blah. Doesn't make it right."

If there's any argument, I can't find one. We've worked enough cases to know the only reason we got the results so fast was because Schock Investigations paid for it.

Thousands of dollars that we'll work extra hours to recoup.

Lucky for Evelyn Jacoby, she has us. "How do you want to handle this?"

"Carefully. We're private investigators not federal agents. And I have no interest in pissing off the Bureau any longer than we have to when it comes to horning in on their case."

On that, we're in agreement. The last thing I want is them

shutting us down. Not when we're making progress. "What are you thinking?"

"We need to share this with Taylor. Evelyn was tied to an FBI investigation and given that this was a cold case, maybe she can hijack it. I don't know. What I do know is that I'm not comfortable with us making a death notice involving someone they're looking for. Dammit."

Dread creeps around inside me. Excitement over the match smothered my logic. Otherwise, it would've occurred to me that Evelyn's family wasn't even aware she'd died. After all this time, they'd probably assumed she had, but assuming it and knowing it, I have to believe, are two different things.

My sister reaches for her phone. Of course she does. "What are you doing?"

"Calling Taylor."

She gives it a final tap and sets it on the desk. A second later, the call connects, the ring filling the office.

"Charlie? How are you? You'd better not be calling me from the hospital."

At this, I smile. Everyone is watching out for my sister.

Charlie rolls her eyes. "I'm in my office with Meg."

"Hi, Taylor." I say. "I filled Charlie in on Evelyn. I also entered the results into GenCo."

"Damn, you women are fast."

I can't argue that. "That's what happens when you're willing to pay. Anyway, I got a match. For Evelyn."

The line goes silent a few long seconds leading me to believe this news has stunned Taylor as much as it did me.

"Come on?" She finally responds. "Really?"

"Yes, ma'am. Appears to be a paternal brother."

"Taylor," Charlie says in her all-business voice, "I'm in no mood to piss off the Bureau, but we need to talk to this guy."

"Not before we do."

Uh-oh. Charlie and Taylor getting into an alpha smackdown—as much fun as that would be to watch—it isn't exactly on my day's wish list. "Both of you, take a breath. We all want the same thing here. Let's figure out how to get this done. Taylor, any chance you can run interference and be the one to talk to Evelyn's brother? It *is* a cold case."

More silence meets my request and if I know anything about her, she's considering the benefits of my suggestion. "Taylor?"

"I'm here. But I'm not sure how I feel about going to my boss with this. I'll have to explain how I identified Evelyn's remains."

Across the desk, I meet my sister's eye and shrug. "Tell him Matt is working a case that got him to her. If he needs more than that, chuck him our way and Charlie will do her magic."

In addition to the sigh that wafts through the phone line, this gets me another eyeroll from the already cranky Charlie.

"Let me see what I can do."

"Fine," Charlie says. "Thank you. And, you know, optimum would be you taking over Evelyn's case, making the death notice and then when you leave, we'll visit her brother."

"That's not asking for much, is it?"

Taylor's sarcasm is not lost on me.

"Not at all." Charlie grins. "Talk to you later."

She taps the screen, cutting off any retort Taylor may have.

Once again, she pushes out of her chair, pausing when she reaches her full height. If she looked pale when I entered, she's downright pasty now.

Her body sways—whoa, there—and I reach across the desk, latching onto her arms.

"Easy. Are you gonna pass out?"

"I'm so damned tired."

"I know. You need rest." Still holding on, I peer over my shoulder. "JJ! Charlie is ready to go home. And don't come in here yelling. She's had a tough day."

A second later, he's rushing in. "Jesus, Charlie. You look like hell."

"Gee," she says, "thanks, honey."

"Don't start," I tell my sister. "Let him take you home. I'll talk to Matt and see what we can do about Taylor."

21

Charlie

*R*ecovering from the accident is more challenging than I anticipated.

I slept terribly, my body aching and my face continuing to swell for hours after JJ took me to his place. It was so tender, I couldn't sleep on my left side and kept waking myself up.

On his way into the office, he dropped me off at home. I'm still in my pjs—a new set he brought me last night and insisted I wear—long after he left. In between a couple short naps, I continue to review files and notes, as well as digging deeper into bank robbers and Evelyn. When Mom calls to check on me, I fill her in on everything.

Including Al's involvement with taking down the London Fog Gang.

I keep circling to him, the case, and what ties Evelyn and Marie might have. JJ confirmed the AG's investigation didn't center on Grenado, only Baez.

Something isn't adding up, and I need to question Al, but since I'm so suspicious he might've been involved in the shooting, I can't bring myself to call him.

I look down at the pink pajamas and sigh over the unicorns on them. JJ is such a big teddy bear, and under his gruff exterior, a total marshmallow when it comes to me. Normally, I wouldn't be caught dead in something like these, but he told me I was his unicorn—that rare, unattainable woman that brings magic to his life.

Cheesy, for sure, but damn if I didn't put them on and wear them with pride. They're surprisingly comfortable, and, even though I wouldn't admit it to anyone, I sort of like them.

I'm debating my next move. There's been no word from the detectives concerning the shooting, and everyone is waiting for me to figure out whether Shock Investigations will run with the Evelyn angle or turn the DNA analysis over to the Bureau. I need to make a decision.

No point in sitting here twiddling my thumbs and rereading notes I've already gone over a dozen times. Nothing new is jumping out at me, and none of it is going to point an obvious finger at who shot up my car yesterday. I need a shower, some makeup, and to get out of the unicorn pajamas. Maybe then I'll have an aha moment and everything will come together.

I leave the notes scattered across my dining room table and shut down my laptop, ready to clean myself up. My doorbell rings and I cringe, praying it's Meg and not someone else. Even with her, I may spend the rest of my life living down these pjs.

Before I get to the door, the person on the other side starts knocking. Faintly, I hear my mother's voice. "Charlize? It's me, mom. Open up."

I seriously consider ignoring her. But I know better. She has a key and will let herself in, then the alarm will go off because she never remembers how to reset it. Things will spiral downward from there. Or she'll grab Meg and they'll come over, because Meg knows I'm home.

When I open the door, I'm horrified that I didn't glance out the peephole first. Not only is Mom on my front doorstep, three other people are with her.

Al, a short Asian gal with glasses and a sprinkling of gray hair amongst the black strands, and another woman who's tall and curvy, with no makeup and a lot of freckles. All three women look excited, Al looks concerned.

Or is it worry?

Four sets of eyes sweep me from head to foot. Not only is it afternoon, but the unicorns probably don't do much to solidify my reputation as a tough former FBI agent and serious private investigator.

"We're here to figure out Gayle and Marie's connection to Evelyn and that gang," Mom says. "This is Clarice and Martha."

That's all the introductions I get as Mom brushes past.

Al follows, the genuine concern on his face giving me pause. "How are you doing?" His gaze lands on my stitches and partial black eye. "Have the police learned anything?"

Clarice and Martha file in, nodding at me as I reply. "Nothing yet. Whoever took the shot was a decent marksman, but not good enough to actually hit me, I guess."

As I say the words, I watch his face for any telltale sign suggesting he was involved.

Nothing in it changes. "A warning, maybe?" He shrugs and shakes his head as if he can't put the pieces together. "I was shocked when your mom told me what happened. Do you think it's tied to this case?" Another probing glance. "I know you have suspects. If I can help, just say the word."

Mom has led the other two into the dining room. They take seats and begin unloading laptops and files.

"I do have a list." I shut the door reluctantly. How in the

world am I going to get these people out of my house? "I promise you'll be the first to know when I'm ready to share it."

It's not much of a veiled threat, but if he's guilty, I expect to see something in his eyes, his composure. Nothing.

He glances over my attire once more and nods, before heading into the dining room. I reset the security system, hang my head for a moment, and consider my options for throwing my mother and her group out. There really aren't any, and I have questions for Al.

He takes a seat at my table. I want to ask where he was yesterday at the time of the shooting, but first, there's something tickling my brain about what Taylor told us regarding the night Sven and his buddies were discovered by Al and Mike. "I understand you worked the London Fog Gang robberies and received an anonymous tip about where they were the night you caught them," I say to him. "Do you remember if the caller was male or female?"

He looks startled at the unexpected questions and leans back. Everyone watches him. "The dispatcher couldn't tell. They had one of those voices that could've been either. Maybe the person was deliberately disguising it. Who knows? The dispatcher attempted to patch them through to me, but the person wouldn't stay on the line."

His hands rest comfortably on the tabletop; his fingers don't fidget. His body language doesn't exhibit any signs of lying. "The caller said to tell me the gang was planning its next heist. They were meeting at an abandoned warehouse in south D.C. within the next few days. My partner and I surveilled the place and the caller was right. We were able to nab them twenty-four hours after the tip came in."

If the snitch was Evelyn and Sven found out, why would he have still showed at that meeting and got caught? But he couldn't have realized it afterwards because he was dead.

My theory there is blown. Evelyn couldn't have been the anonymous tipster.

I move on to my second question. "Sven and his gang were living under false identities, according to several reports. Apparently, the IDs were done by a professional. Did you ever track down who created them?"

I see the corners of his eyes narrow ever so slightly. "They had plenty of money and connections in the underground. Could've been anyone."

All eyes shift to me. "Any chance your tipster was the person supplying them?"

Like a tennis match, the audience's eyes go to Al. "I doubt it. How would a forger know about their comings and goings?"

Because perhaps, every time they planned a heist, they had their forger prepped and ready. I don't say the words out loud, but the women around my table are smart. I see the gears turning in Mom's head.

"I suppose it's a long shot," I concede. "I was just wondering if the person doing it for them could've been an artist?"

A long, pregnant pause. "In the digital age? Even back then, forging signatures was rarely necessary and ID theft wasn't unusual. Is there someone in particular you're thinking might have been involved?"

He knows exactly who I'm thinking of. Mom does, too. "Marie?" she volunteers.

"It's one of the possibilities we should look at."

She makes a note and glances up. "Can we get some coffee?"

"I haven't made any."

She looks aghast. Pushing away from the table, she tosses her glasses on the notepad. "Well, we're going to need it, and you look like you could use a whole pot yourself."

Thanks, Mom. Reluctantly, I follow her and pull down the

coffee bag while she fills the carafe with water. "Is this necessary?" I ask, quietly. "I'm not exactly up for company."

She takes the bag from my hand and begins scooping grounds into the maker. "I knew you'd want to talk to Al about his connection to the gang. You might want to change your clothes before we dig in."

It's all I can do not to get my hackles up, but I notice she looks tired around the eyes. "How are you feeling today?" I ask. "Did you sleep okay last night?"

The battle armor she's wearing slips a little. "Actually, I didn't sleep well at all. Your dad was snoring, and I kept seeing the accident over and over in my mind. If either of those bullets had connected..." Her hands pause in mid-air, gaze dropping to the bag of grounds. I don't miss the tremble in her voice. "Charlie, we've stumbled into something big. I feel it. This has gotten more dangerous than I expected."

She believes she's on the trail of a serial killer, but watching him from behind her blinds and being shot at are two very different things.

Her gaze rises to meet mine. "Do you think it's safe to move forward? There's nothing I want more than to figure out this mystery, but if it means putting you or Meg in danger..."

She trails off, a question left dangling. I rub her arm. "We've definitely stepped in some shit, Mom. Yes, it's dangerous, and yes, things could get worse before they get better. Meg and I know how to take care of ourselves. I would feel better if you backed down and let us handle it."

The defiant light returns. "I'm not asking you to charge into the fire without me. I started this, and I'll finish it."

"Okay then. But we proceed with caution, and do this the right way."

"I thought we were."

I motion for her to follow me to my room. Once there, I close the door for added privacy. "We came by the painting of

Evelyn illegally," I remind her. "I'm going to turn the information about her over to Taylor and the FBI and let them proceed to investigate that angle. They can close out Evelyn's missing persons case, which they didn't care much about, except for the fact she might've known where the money was. Beyond that, I have to figure out how to prove the connection between her and Marie, and possibly Gayle, without using the portrait."

She lowers her voice, now my co-conspirator. "Gayle got a new security system installed. I saw a van there yesterday, and it looks like they have trip wires, spotlights, and cameras everywhere now. I saw the installer showing Gayle how it all works."

No surprise after we were almost caught by him that night. He never saw us, but he must suspect somebody was messing around and decided not to take any chances.

"If only I could get into the house and look for something that connects Marie and Evelyn," Mom says, "then we could get the FBI to reopen the case and figure out if Marie and Gayle were involved in the bank robberies, or know something about Evelyn's death."

I'm convinced Sven killed Evelyn and buried her body with the others—he probably killed them as well—if only I could figure out why. Mom, however, still believes Gayle is our killer.

"We can't go back and snoop around. Even if we found a solid piece of evidence, it would be thrown out in court. You understand that, right, Mom? And if you buddy up to Marie and start asking questions about Evelyn? That could open a whole other can of worms. I don't want you anywhere near her or Gayle. Please, for me."

Her excitement fades. "What about Meg? She already has a sort of friendship with Marie. Maybe she could go over under the pretense of talking art and snoop around."

Heaven help me. If Marie and Gayle are dangerous, I'm not throwing my sister into their lair. "I'll figure it out." I open the door. "I just need time to think through how we're going to find the evidence."

Mom returns to the kitchen to finish the coffee, and I'm looking for my usual outfit of slacks and a blouse, when my doorbell rings again.

Damn it. Who is it, now?

Maybe Meg saw Mom pull in and has come over to join us. I consider letting Mom answer the door, but under the circumstances, I don't want more visitors outside of my sister, and Mom will let anyone in. After the shooting, and the fact that one of my suspects is sitting in my dining room, I'm a little on edge.

"Do you want me to get that?" Mom calls.

I burst from the bedroom and practically run to the front of the house. "I've got it! Don't answer the door!"

I'm damned if I do and damned if I don't answer it myself, I realize. This time, however, I look out the peephole.

It's not Meg on my doorstep, but the last person I want to see right now.

Taylor Sinclair is standing there with an older guy, looking as uncomfortable as I feel. I have the sinking feeling I know why they're here.

I glance at my pjs, thinking about the fact I need to run a brush through my hair, and the left side of my face looks like I was in a bar fight.

Mom comes up behind me. "Who is it?" she half-whispers.

I snap out of my mental conundrum. "The Feds."

"Oh, no! What do they want?"

"Nothing good."

Opening the door, I use my surprising attire and body to block them from looking in. "Agent Sinclair," I say professionally. "What are you doing here?"

Her shoulders are stiff, chin up. She's all agent, but her eyes apologize. A hand motions at the man slightly behind her and to the left. "This is Assistant Agent in Charge, Jeremy Lind. My boss."

Lind puts his hands on the belt at his waist. The heat of the day is making him sweat, and he's a good thirty pounds over-weight, which isn't helping. He's no taller than Taylor, bald, and his sunglasses show me unicorns in their mirrored reflection.

"Ms. Schock." He's chewing gum, and smacks it, before he says, "We want to close this case pronto, and it's important we notify next of kin. I'm told you've identified someone related to Evelyn Jacoby? We'd like the DNA report and the information on this relative."

The earlier feeling of my hackles rising returns. I was already planning to turn this information over to them, but this feels like they're piggybacking on our work to make their job a whole lot easier.

I glance at Taylor, an accusation, but her face pleads with me to cooperate. She wouldn't shut us out completely if she was in charge, but Lind will.

A fight requires more energy than I have today, yet I can't help but borrow some of Mom's battle armor. "I'm happy to share it, Special Agent Lind, as long as my sister can be there to ask questions concerning our investigation in regards to who Jacoby was friends with."

A door slams and Meg strides over, as if she's ready to join the discussion.

Lind smacks his gum and smiles as if I'm dense and he has to explain things to me. "Your investigation,"—he says the word with disdain, letting me know he finds being a PI a long fall from an FBI agent—"is not our concern. You're free to talk to this brother at any time, but only after we've interviewed him. You understand we're still looking into the disappearance of nearly a million dollars and if there's any chance he knows something, it's important we get to him first."

Not only is Mom looking over my shoulder, I sense Al

joining her. Taylor and Lind's gazes stray to a spot behind me. There's an exchange of nods. Meg's body language goes into defense mode.

Lind continues, the smacking and smiling growing annoying enough, I wish his bald head would explode. "Ms. Schock." He makes sure not to call me *former agent* or *doctor*—both titles I've earned—in order to put me in my place again. "I'm instructing you to stay clear of Evelyn Jacoby's family member or you'll face charges for interfering in a federal case."

Mom sucks in a breath, Meg glances at me. Al says, "That's not necessary, ASAC Lind, is it? We're not interfering with your investigation, and we'd appreciate it if you don't interfere with ours. After all, the Schock sisters are the ones who've done the legwork for you. A little professional courtesy would be nice."

To say I'm shocked that Al's taking our side is an under-statement. There's a part of me that still likes this guy, no matter how hard I try not to. My suspicion he's behind the shooting dims.

Out on the street, I realize Mom's bodyguard, Tony, has been watching this whole show from his truck. He must've followed her and Al, and I'm glad he's keeping a close eye on her, but I'm equally dismayed all of these people have seen me in these damn pajamas. It's hard to convey the true Charlie-Schock-I'm-in-charge attitude while everyone keeps getting distracted by the fact I'm dressed like a three-year-old.

The least of my worries, right?

To top things off, a blue Mustang pulls up and there's Matt. One more to join the party. I wonder if he knew Taylor was being forced to come here with Lind and take the DNA analysis.

My sister steps around Taylor so she can stand shoulder to shoulder with me. We both face Lind, a united front. "We don't have to share anything with you," she says bluntly. "Unless you have a warrant or something, right Charlie?"

From inside, comes another voice, one of the Citizens Solving Cold Cases calls out, agreeing with Meg. "Tell them, sister!"

"You're not stealing my case!" Mom says with self-righteous determination.

Matt jogs up the sidewalk, consternation on his face as he surveys the confrontation. I take a deep breath and project every ounce of my true personality, regardless of my clothes, face, or the fact I used to be an agent and believe in teamwork. "Meg, Al, Mom, everyone inside."

Lind turns to watch Matt approach Taylor. Meg pushes the others back.

Matt's gaze bounces between me, Taylor, and Lind. "Nice pjs. What's going on?"

I would never insist he cross the picket line, so to speak. His loyalty has to lie with Taylor, no matter what she's being forced to do at the moment. I ignore his question, and in my pink unicorn pajamas, with my chin up, I do something really stupid.

"If you want a copy of Evelyn Jacoby's analysis and the information regarding her next of kin," I say to Lind, "then I suggest you fill out the paperwork to request a sample of her DNA be run through your system. That should only take, what? A couple weeks, maybe a month? Then, when you can upload them to one of the ancestry programs like GenCo, you'll find the information about her brother. Until then, unless you get a warrant, we're not sharing jack shit. Unless, as previously stated, you work *with* us and allow my sister to interview Ms. Jacoby's brother when you meet with him."

Stepping back inside with a slight flourish of unicorns, I shut the door on Lind and Taylor's shocked faces.

22

Meg

$\mathcal{I}$'m waiting on Eric Bronson's front porch while Taylor and Lind give him the news about Evelyn. After Charlie's refusal, Lind reconsidered his options, figured it more expedient to strike a deal with us, and knocked on my sister's door.

His deal included Matt and I tagging along. Now, wanting to give Mr. Bronson privacy, we've opted to stay outside.

I hate this. I don't know what the relationship was between Eric and Evelyn, but for nearly twenty years he's been waiting, wondering where she might be.

Today, he'll have his answer. Right now in fact, he's being informed his sister's body was dumped and discarded, in a cold, damp hole.

At least Evelyn Jacoby will have a proper burial.

I peer up at the sky, a brilliant blue that reminds me, even if

I struggle to believe it some days, there is a God and beauty does exist in a harsh world.

"Tough day," Matt says.

He's seated on the top step, an elbow propped on his knee, chin in hand.

"I'm trying to imagine what it feels like. Not knowing where your sister is."

"Taylor is the perfect person to deliver this news."

He's right. As a child, Taylor's sister had gone missing and was held captive by a psycho until Taylor found her last year. All that time. Lost.

So, yes, Taylor has a level of understanding none of us can relate to.

The front door of the nineteen thirty-ish two-story home swings open. I turn back to where Lind holds the door for Taylor.

She steps onto the porch, her gaze immediately going to Matt who offers one solid nod. If I know him at all, he's fighting the urge to wrap her in his arms. He's good like that. Always on alert when the women in his life need a shoulder to lean on. Or a hug.

Taylor simply nods back. She's a pro and I suspect she won't tolerate coddling in front of her boss. No matter how much she might need it.

Behind her, a man—Bronson probably—appears. The profile Charlie pulled advised us he turned sixty-three recently. His full head of gray hair and the sagging skin under his eyes reflect every one of them—if not more.

His gaze shifts from me, still standing at the rail, to Matt, now on his feet.

Bronson gives a curt nod. "Hello. I'm Eric Bronson."

I move closer, angling around Lind who seems to have taken root. I offer my hand. "Meg Schock. I'm so sorry for your loss." I gesture to Matt. "And this is my associate, Matt Stephens."

The two exchange a silent greeting and Bronson brings his attention back to me. "Thank you. I figured after all these years she was...gone, but..." He takes a second, closes his eyes and breathes.

"There's always hope," I add.

He opens his eyes. "Yeah. So much for that."

Lind finally moves. He reaches into his inside jacket pocket and produces a business card, handing it to Bronson. "If you think of anything, give us a call. And again, I'm sorry to bring you bad news."

Bronson takes it and flicks a finger against it. "Thanks."

Taylor says her goodbyes and the two head toward their Bureau car parked at the curb.

"Mr. Bronson," I say, "I'm not sure how much Agents Lind and Sinclair told you, but we're from Schock Investigations. We're private investigators. Well, Matt and my sister are. I'm a forensic sculptor who helps with cold cases. I know this is a bad time, but we're working on one we think somehow involves your sister."

Bronson steps back. "Come in. I don't know what I can tell you, but maybe you can help me find out what happened."

We walk into a small and efficiently tidy living room. A leather recliner sits adjacent to a patchwork sofa with a fuchsia hand-knit blanket draped over it. My artist's eye can't help but notice the craftsmanship.

"That's a lovely blanket."

"My wife. They're all over the house. She was in the middle of one for Ev when she went missing." He glances up the stairs, then puffs his cheeks, blowing out air. "That damn thing has been in the guest room all this time. I guess we'll bury it with her, so she'll finally have it."

The words are a kick to my chest. This poor man. All these

years he's been in limbo, waiting to hear something—anything —from his sister. Now, it's over and he'll have to work through the emotions that come with the grieving process.

Or, maybe his is already done. Either way, his need for answers on how she died will continue. Perhaps we can help with that.

One thing at a time...

He waves us to the sofa. "Have a seat. Can I get you anything? Water, iced tea?"

We shake our heads and settle in. On the coffee table is an overstuffed photo album. One of those old three-ring binder styles that's bursting with ribbons and yellowing paper.

Bronson gestures to it as he drops into his recliner. "I was showing the FBI folks some pictures." He leans in and pushes it to us. "This is Ev's. They wanted to take it, but I told them to come back. Now that I know she's...well...I want to look through it. Ah, damn. She's been gone twenty years. You'd think it wouldn't be a surprise." He points at the album. "You can open it. If you want."

The offer paralyzes me. If Charlie were here, she'd be halfway through by now. Her experience has taught her the correct coping skills when faced with heartbreak. Me? I don't have a clue what I should do so I glance at Matt, giving him my wide-eyed help-me stare.

Taking his cue, he reaches for the binder, dragging it closer and opening it.

On the first page are random photos of a young woman with blonde-streaked light brown hair. She's sitting on bleachers and waving a pom-pom. Football game. High school perhaps? College? I really have no idea.

From what I remember of the painting and photo I've seen, it has to be Evelyn. Her hair isn't as dark, but it's clearly high-lighted in these photos.

Matt scans more pages, all containing pictures of the same

woman. Christmas, Halloween and what looked like St. Patrick's Day.

"She liked parties," Mr. Bronson tells us.

I point to a photo of the woman with the blonde-streaked hair. "This is her?"

"Yeah."

Matt turns another and there's Evelyn, in front of a Welcome to Niagara Falls sign. A second picture shows her with a man.

"That's her boyfriend. Chris Svenson."

Mr. Bronson's words are simple, but that flat, monotone sound conveys so much more.

Matt glances up. "You weren't a fan?"

"From the get-go something was off. I sure as hell didn't know he was a criminal. When Ev left with him, I figured she'd be back. That it was a temporary thing. She said she wanted to travel. See the country. How the hell did I know her boyfriend was robbing banks?"

I check out another page. All Evelyn and Chris. "How did you find out?"

"The night he got killed. I saw his picture on the news. About had a stroke."

"Did you think she was involved?" Matt asks.

"I was more worried she might've gotten killed along with him. I called the FBI right away. It took them a day to get back to me. Imagine that? A whole damned day. I told the agent who contacted me she was Svenson's girlfriend. They said it looked like she'd bugged out. That if I heard from her, I was to call them. Eventually, they told me the cash was still missing. They thought she took off with it. Maybe left the country."

I try to imagine what that might feel like and cannot. Listening to a federal agent tell you your sister has absconded with stolen money from multiple bank robberies.

"Did you ever hear from her?"

"No. But I also didn't think she took it. It wasn't her style. And she'd lived with our parents until she met Svenson. What did she know about being on her own *and* on the run? She'd never even paid an electric bill."

The room falls silent and Matt turns another page. I'm thankful for the distraction as I'm not quite sure what to say next. I skim the left side. More photos of Evelyn and Svenson. I remind myself to check for bank robberies in Niagara Falls. See if the dates match what's on the photos. I move to the next page and—hello—a photo of Evelyn and another woman, a platinum blonde stops me cold.

Three photos.

The women at a bonfire. They're smiling and holding paper cups up in a toast. In one, Evelyn beams, the light from the fire reflecting her luminous skin. She looks absolutely ethereal while the woman next to her is...not. In her I sense a hardness. Her smile, although wide, hits me more as a tight sneer.

Dimple. Left cheek.

I move closer, then finally lift the binder so I can study the album. And dimple.

The platinum blond hair—and something else, the eyes maybe— throw me off, but...her.

Across from us, Mr. Bronson shifts, craning his neck to see what captured my attention. "That's her friend. Mary. They went to high school together."

Mary.

Marie.

The names are so close. If this was indeed Marie, would she have taken a name so similar to her own while living on the run?

"Mary," Matt says, "huh. Did she, by any chance, leave with Evelyn?"

Bronson nods. "Yeah. She was dating one of Svenson's buddies. That was a big part of it. They wanted to see the country and figured they'd do it together." He circles his hand in the air. "My sister and her romantic dreams. She figured it'd be some kind of fairy tale. Her best friend on the road with her."

Romantic dreams notwithstanding, in my twenties, I'd have done it. Just taken off to see the world. Crazy how life changes us, forces us to grow up. "Where's Mary now?"

Bronson shrugs. "No idea. She went missing with Evelyn. Last I heard, the FBI was looking for both of 'em."

As soon as we arrive back at the office, I close my door, tell Haley only to enter if someone is dead and settle in at my desk. I borrowed a couple photos of Mary from Mr. Bronson, promising to return them tomorrow.

I need them for an age progression.

My office is blissfully quiet and I close my eyes for a solid minute, centering myself and rolling the tension from my shoulders.

Typically, I'll play classical music while I work, but today, for whatever reason, silence calls to me. I go with it and lay the photos of Marie in front of me, studying the various expressions. A smile, a frown, drawn in brows that, over time, if repeated enough, will leave their stamp.

I grab my favorite sketchpad and pencil and draw a circle in the center of the page. Underneath, I quickly add the chin, cheeks and jawline. It's not perfect, but I don't need that.

Guidelines down the center and across the face come next. I glance at the photos, then add almond shaped eyes, skinny eyebrows, and a narrow nose.

In minutes, my basic outline is complete. I check the hair. Platinum blonde. I rough in the hairline, giving my subject long silky strands similar to the photo.

I should hand these to Jerome. Let him do this. He's not as advanced in age progressions, but he'd have no preconceived ideas of where he might be headed. I'm impatient though and

MISTY EVANS & ADRIENNE GIORDANO

refuse to waste time driving. Instead, I force myself to put Marie's face from my mind.

On the page, I add lines across the forehead then sketch in crow's feet and a few more subtle wrinkles here and there. Bags under the eyes wouldn't be out of the question. I add them. Not too heavy, just a bit.

With age, a woman's skin loses its elasticity, causing thin lines. Muscle flexibility also decreases leading to drooping jowls. In extreme cases, it appears taut over bone. Marie isn't that old so I simply trim the cheeks, sharpening the edges.

Now the mouth. I rough in vertical lines above the top lip, then a few more crescent ones at the corners and a bit of sagging.

I tweak the lips, giving them less volume, then tweak some more, erasing and redrawing.

Erase.

Draw.

Erase.

Draw.

I lose myself in the process, allowing my instincts to guide me. I can't unsee Marie, but I have the photos of Mary to work with so I keep at it, sneaking peeks while I add fine details.

I finally set my sketchpad down and check the clock. I've been at it over an hour, but something is missing. The mouth. What is it? Come on, come on.

I go back to the photos. Concentrate on Mary's. In the third picture, she smiles wide and...bam. There it is.

Dimple.

Left cheek.

I add it and set my pencil down again. Beside my sketchpad. Where Marie's face stares back at me.

164

23

Charlie

*T*he heat is in the normal July range as I pull into the front lot. I'm driving a loaner my insurance company provided and it's a far cry from my beautiful BMW.

I feel lighter this morning, grateful that Meg and Matt went to do the interview with Eric, along with Taylor and Lind. I haven't heard from either of them yet.

Haley buzzes me in and I'm surprised to find a man in one of the chairs near the window. He rockets to his feet, shorter than I am, thanks to my heels. His hair is white-blond and his skin tan, I'm guessing from many days on the golf course. He introduces himself and offers his hand. Al's former partner.

I shake and accept several message slips from Haley. Mike Grenado checks me over, pausing on my stitches and partial black eye. "What's the other guy look like?" he teases.

His smile shows a set of perfectly white teeth, though I

sense he's uneasy being here. "When I catch him," I say, watching his face carefully, "he'll be worse than this, I guarantee."

He chuckles nervously. "I wanted to personally apologize for standing you up." He points at his mouth. "A broken tooth sent me for an emergency visit to the dentist. I meant to stop by afterwards, but the pain meds made me woozy."

I don't believe him, but I also don't know him, so I give him the benefit of the doubt. "Come back to my office. Haley, would you get Mr. Grenado some coffee, or perhaps he'd like water?"

She starts to rise, but he puts out a hand. "Don't bother. I'm on my way to another appointment." He winks at our receptionist then smiles at me. "I just wanted to reiterate that Al's a great guy. That's what you were wanting to know, isn't it? Is he trying to get a job or something with you?"

"What makes you think that?"

A lift and fall of his shoulders. "You're a PI, former Bureau, right? Saw you and your sister on the news. Figured he's looking for work."

"Was he a good partner?"

His lips thin. "Absolutely. The best. Once he's on your side, he'll do anything for you. A real team player."

I ignore the fact he's anxious to leave. "You ever have any disagreements over cases? Any doubts about his actions on the job?"

The tightening around the corners of his eyes is so slight, it's barely noticeable. "Sure, we disagreed sometimes. Don't all partners?" This is the truth. "But Al was an outstanding agent. Best close rate in the business. Loyal to a fault."

That's the party line.

If I'm gonna get anything worthwhile out of this guy, I need to keep him off balance. I switch gears. "Did you enjoy being an agent?"

The smile grows, but I can see he's trying to figure out why I'm asking all these questions. "I loved it."

Another truth. "You retired shortly after Al, is that correct?"

The corner of his right eye twitches ever so slightly. "Wasn't the same without him. Knew there'd never be anyone who watched out for me the way he did." Truth.

He glances toward the door again, returns to me. "I tell you, Dr. Schock, once Al is your friend, you never worry about whose got your back."

I feel the same way regarding my sister. She'd cover for me, no matter what I did, even if I broke the law. She'd break it for me without blinking an eye. Take a bullet for me.

And I would for her.

"Do *anything* for you," I emphasize, repeating his earlier words. Would Al cover for him if he was involved in illegal activities? I itch to ask, but I know that'd send him out the door before my next breath.

He glances at his watch—a Rolex similar to JJ's. "Sorry," he says. "I really have to run."

He's not getting away from me that easily. "Do you remember Chris Svenson and the London Fog Gang?"

He pulls up short. Glances out the window as if wishing he were anywhere but here. "Vaguely."

A notorious bank robbery gang he killed several members of and that's his answer? Haley shoots me a look, suggesting she's listening intently to every word and doubts his sincerity as much as I do.

I lean on her desk and cross my ankles. "My team uncovered the identity of a woman left in the Virginia woods near Whitetop Mountain. Turns out to be Sven's longtime girlfriend, Evelyn Jacoby."

Wariness crosses his face. "Is that so? Good for you." He gives me a nod and reaches for the handle.

"I looked up the first robbery Svenson committed, back in his hometown. It was just him then. He didn't have a gang."

Grenado has the door cracked open, ready to make his escape. Hot air rushes in, pooling around my pumps. His right eye twitches again when he glances at me.

Gotcha. "Eyewitnesses saw him leave the bank and jump in a stolen blue Celica," I continue, combing my memory for details. "They found the car a couple weeks later at a rock quarry, right? No one could identify the driver at the scene of the robbery, but one of the folks who went to church with Svenson's parents mentioned Chris and a buddy were always together. Chris's friend, what was his name? Jan, wasn't it?"

The fact it was an ambiguous name like Gayle is actually what caught my attention late last night when I couldn't sleep and reread the stacks of notes on my table once more. "The kid had an alibi that weekend— he was in college forty miles away. Ring any bells?" I ask. "Funny though, Jan apparently dropped out shortly after Sven disappeared, never showed up again."

Grenado shrugs, not releasing his hold. "So?"

In the back of my mind, I'm annoyed he's wasting our precious cool air. Haley is too—she adjusts her fan with obvious motions. "Who was the driver for the London Fog Gang?"

He turns slightly toward his escape. "They took turns, I guess."

This is a lie; I see it in his posture. "Four guys with varying skill sets from hacking and security evasion to lock picking, and they didn't have a designated driver?"

His expression is a forced blank. He doesn't answer, but releases the door and it closes with a soft *snick.*

"Did you check into that angle?" I ask, casual as can be.

His posture becomes defensive, hands clenching into fists before sinking into his pockets. He throws his chest out. All classic signs he's hiding something. "Al did and came up dry."

I tap the slips against my leg and appear perplexed. "Huh. I spoke to him yesterday when he was at my house and he claimed *you* did but found nothing."

Two can play the lying game, but he doesn't know I'm bluffing. The phone rings and Haley reaches for it like a lifeline. "Schock Investigations," she says in her professional voice.

My suspect rocks back on his heels. "It was a long time ago. My memory's faulty. I can't remember every element of every case."

Definitely lying. Not about remembering specific details about cases—hell, I've forgotten more than I remember. He's lying about who checked the getaway driver angle.

He did.

Which means, maybe he's lying about other things. What if Al wasn't the one entrapping people? What if it was Mike? And Al—who'd do anything for him—covered it up.

But which one got to the snitch who was going to tell all to the Justice Department?

Haley says, "Yes, she's here, but she's in a meeting, Mrs. Schock."

I glance over and she looks at me with consternation as she listens to my mom's reply.

"Nice meeting you." Grenado throws open the door. "Good luck with your case."

He bolts, and swearing under my breath, I wiggle my fingers at Haley. She hands me the phone, relieved.

Mom is still speaking. "...tell her, I'm taking Marie a coffee cake. A neighborly gesture and an apology for being so nosy all this time. I'll let her know what I find out."

"You are absolutely not going over there," I inform her.

"Charlie?"

"Mom, we're turning everything over to the FBI later this afternoon. We believe Marie is a person of interest in an open case, albeit a cold one."

Not to mention the fact Gayle could be one of the LFG.

"Charlie?" This comes from behind me. Meg. She holds up a drawing in one hand, a picture of a woman in the other.

"Hang on a sec, Mom," I say, covering the receiver. To Meg, "Is that who I think it is?"

She's done a hasty age progression, but it's spot on. She nods. "I need to send this to Taylor." Excitement ripples through me. By golly, we've got a solid tie between Marie and Evelyn. "Things are breaking open," I happily report. "But it's time to let the FBI take over and investigate Marie and Gayle."

Mom huffs. "They'll blow it," she says, matter-of-factly. "I understand and respect you're the expert when it comes to this, but the FBI isn't invested like I am. They don't understand. It's my case, Charlize. Please don't give them my notes. They'll screw it up!"

Meg offers the drawing to Haley, who shakes her head. "Fax isn't working," she says. "I can scan it and email it to Taylor."

Meg glances at me. I chuck the messages on the desk and grab the portrait. I'll take it to Taylor in person with the rest of the files I've compiled for her. "I'm sorry, but we agreed, remember? This is the right thing to do, Mom."

Dead silence.

Meg is so much better at handling her than I am. I motion at my sister, then the phone. She adamantly mouths "no."

"Your investigation is about to solve multiple cases," I say to appease her. "We've identified Evelyn, we've brought closure to her brother. We've linked Marie to her, and possibly the London Fog Gang. I believe we have circumstantial evidence connecting Gayle to the bank robberies as well. If he and Marie were involved and know where the missing money is, that could be another matter that gets closed, all because of *you*."

There's a long, pregnant pause. She's thinking it over, debating whether to continue arguing or take this win and let the FBI close it out. She's spent years on it, and I understand her hesitation to turn it over to someone else. Especially the FBI, who obviously didn't do everything they could in the first place, thanks to Al and Mike.

"If you'd like to go with us," I offer, "I'm sure Taylor would appreciate your input."

She stalls, then finally says, "Fine. But I'll need a ride. My car is still in the garage."

"Meg will pick you up," I volunteer and my sister grabs a pencil from Haley's desk and throws it at me. "Give her twenty minutes."

"Charlize." Her reproving tone is one I know well. I heard it hundreds of times growing up. "I appreciate all you and Meg have done, and it pains me to do this, but..."

Another pause and a heavy intake of breath.

"Mom," I start, "do not go over to Ga—"

"You're fired," she says.

And then she hangs up.

I stare at the dead phone a second before I hand it to Haley. The security system goes off and Matt enters, waving down the hall. "Sorry, H," he calls to Haley. "I'll reset it."

She hangs up the receiver, and flips Matt the bird.

Head spinning, I raise a hand to fend off Meg's litany of complaints about taking Mom with us to see Taylor. "I know. I'm sorry, but I think we have something more critical to worry about at the moment."

"What?" Meg asks.

"What?" Matt echoes, joining us.

I fill them in on what Mom originally told me she was going to do, and the fact she just fired us. "I don't think she has any intention of going to the Bureau with us. She's about to do something stupid, and I need you to intercept her."

My sister laughs without humor over the fact we're fired, then turns serious. "She could be in real danger, Charlie."

"I'll call Dad, you two head to their house. I need to get this picture to Taylor."

Meg's already on her way to grab her purse. Matt's on her heels.

"I'll drive," he says.

A minute later, they run out the back door.

24

Meg

My mother is starting to piss me off. Lucky for her, Matt and I are joined at the hip on this case so he's available to help me on this trip to my parents'. Plus... Marie. I have no idea what to do about her. I should've given the age progression assignment to Jerome. What the hell was I thinking? My knowledge of Marie could've guided the sketch.

It's not too late, though. When we get back, I'll swing by his place. Ask him to do the sketch and see what he comes up with. If they're close, then we'll at least know Marie is more-than-likely Mary.

I grab Matt, telling him to drive while I close my eyes for a couple of minutes to focus.

It's just not the day to kill our mother.

It's not.

I'm usually the Zen one.

This? It's taxing me.

Matt swings the Mustang into my parents' driveway. The garage is closed and my dad's car, that usually sits outside, is gone. Who knows where he might be?

I bolt from the car, charging across the pristine lawn that glistens in the morning sun.

The door is locked so I use my key then yell for my mother. No answer.

"Damn her," I mutter. "Of all the fool things."

I stomp back to find Matt casually leaning against the car. "What's up?"

I start toward the road. "No one's home. She must be over there already."

"I'll come with you."

Ha. That's all I need for this shitshow. Without stopping, I hold one hand up. "I've got this. If we all pile in there, they'll be suspicious. Stay close. In case we need you."

"Meg—"

"I know. Believe me. I'd love to drag you in there with me but..." What? What kind of insanity is this that a forensic sculptor is chasing down suspected bank robbers? "Swear to God, I need a new career."

Behind me, I hear Matt snort. "We all say that."

Oh, no. No, sir. I am not one of them. Matt and Charlie live for this stuff. A good, juicy homicide? They'll take it twenty-four seven. Me? I want green tea and the feel of sticky clay in my hands.

As I approach, my chest is so tight I might burst. Damn, my mother. I'll probably have a heart attack before I even get to the door.

And me without a pot brownie.

I steal a glance behind me where Matt has wandered and is now on the sidewalk in front of Gayle's. I should tell him to go back, that his presence is suspicious, but—no. I have no idea what I'm walking into. From where he's standing, if I scream, he'll hear me.

Such a pleasant thought.

Before knocking, I press my ear to the door. Not a peep.

Maybe Mom didn't come over?

Or maybe, at this very second, they're carving up her body.

I bang a little harder than necessary, but whatever. If she's being butchered someone is getting their ass kicked. I'm small, but mighty.

The door swings open and Gayle stands there while a blast of cool air from inside reaches me. For a moment, I'm stunned. Frozen on the doorstep. In all the conversations we've had about Gayle, the weird guy across the street, this is the closest I've come physically. It's a good thing my legs won't move. If they could, I'd take a giant step back. He studies me a second with dull brown eyes that hold...nothing. Just a bland stare that knocks me even more on edge. A weird energy wraps around me, sending a chill straight up my neck.

I have no idea if this guy is a bank robber, serial killer or what, but he hasn't spoken a word and I already know I can't stay anywhere near him.

The silence lingers until he finally holds his hands out and cranes his neck toward me. "Help you?"

"I'm, uh, Meg." I point over my shoulder. "My parents live across the street. Is my mom here? She told my sister she was bringing over a coffee cake."

"They're in the kitchen. You people can't keep dropping in. We like our privacy."

Dick.

Head.

She brings him a damned cake and now he's being rude? Really?

"Oh, o-kay. I'll tell her not to be nice anymore."

He fires a grunt my way—my set down not lost on him—and swivels, signaling me to follow.

I step inside then peek outside where Matt is still on the sidewalk. Gayle doesn't seem too concerned about closing his front door, so I leave it open.

Just in case.

On my way down the short, wallpapered hallway, I pass a neat, sparsely decorated living room. There's a plaid sofa with the requisite oak coffee table and a brown leather side chair with a glass cocktail table beside it. The whole package is a mishmash of material and textures.

The kitchen is equally odd. A farm table with two white, ladder back chairs and a set of mismatched chairs on the other side.

Ohmygod. They must be all garage sale finds and that completely wigs me out. Who knows where that furniture came from?

I shove my shoulders back, force myself to focus. Mental chaos is never good for me. It spins into a panic attack and that's about the dead last thing I want right now.

"Meg," Mom chirps, "what a lovely surprise. We're just about to have cake."

Marie stands at the counter, knife in hand. Prickles shoot up my neck. Does she really need a carving knife for a coffee cake?

"Well, hello, Meg," she says. "So nice to see you. Join us."

The words are friendly, but there's a flatness to them. Or maybe I'm freaking the hell out.

Gayle leans against the counter, folding his arms while his lifeless brown eyes stay pinned to me.

"No. Thank you," I tell Marie. "Mom, we should go, I need your help with something."

She waves me off. "Oh nonsense. It can wait."

"Actually, no. It can't. It's...Charlie. She needs us." Using her as bait, particularly after she got shot, is dirty pool, but I'm a desperate woman. I face Marie. "My mother and sister were in a car accident. Charlie is in rough shape so it's all hands on deck." I swing my arms toward the living room. "Let's go, Mom. Chop-chop."

A noise—the quiet footfall of rubber on tile—draws me around. Alfonzo Baez is walking toward me with Matt in tow.

What in holy hell is going on?

"What is it?"

This from Gayle who's now on my right, bringing all his negative energy with him. He peers down the hallway, spots Al and his head snaps backward.

In my line of work, I've seen enough shocked faces to recognize one and Gayle? Stunned. Blown to bits.

And, if I'm not mistaken, the way his shoulders hunch, there's a little fear thrown in.

I shift my gaze to Al, then to Gayle and back to Al. "What's going on?"

"What..." Gayle stutters, "are you doing here?"

Wait one second. Could they...? Do they...? I waggle my finger between them. "Do you two know each other?"

Mom steps up behind me, peering right over my shoulder, further crowding the doorway. I've got Gayle on one side and now Mom on the other and between the two of them they're an absolute medley of weird energy.

"Al?" Mom asks. "Is that you?"

It's him all right.

Al meets her eye and blows out a breath. "Helen, what are you doing? Are you okay?"

Gayle pushes around me and pokes his finger at Matt. "Who the hell are you? I want all you nosey people out."

Ever the calm one, Matt holds up his hands. "Whoa, dude. Relax. I'm a friend of Meg's. This guy showed up and I figured I'd check on her. No harm. No foul."

"Yeah, well, get out."

"We'll go," Al says quickly. "Helen, come on."

Mom turns and speaks to Marie, but the words are a blur. I'm stuck on Gayle asking Al what he's doing here. There's something about the way he said it. Baez and my mother have been working together a long time. And Al was an FBI agent prior to that. Twenty years, Charlie told me. He'd worked the London Fog bank robbery case. Charlie shared that, too. But this is different. It's as if they've met. A familiarity that puzzles me.

My thoughts speed up, racing too fast for me to decipher, but one question breaks free.

If Gayle and Marie are somehow connected to this gang and the FBI is still looking for all that money, how has Al, with all of his Bureau contacts, not alerted someone there about the strange couple living across the street from my mother?

Even if he didn't suspect they might be part of the bank robberies, he's been actively investigating them. His first call should've been to some federal agent friend to run a background check on them.

That's what Charlie would do.

And now I want to know why, after all this time, he hasn't.

"Al," I wait a beat for him to focus on me. When he does, I hold his stare, making sure he knows I'm done messing around and want answers. "How do you know these people?"

25

Charlie

*M*att's text comes in while I'm driving and talking to Taylor on my Bluetooth. Taylor can't meet until three, so I decided to join Meg and Matt and try talking sense to Mom.

Meg and Mom are both at Gayle's, it reads. *Directive?*

At Gayle's? This news makes me accelerate and swerve around a Subaru filled with kids, probably on their way to the local pool. The loaner's air conditioning drops a notch as the car shifts, blowing warm air instead of cold.

Taylor is in my ear saying, "I need to talk to Al before I go to Gayle and Marie. As soon as I'm done with this meeting, I'll call him."

I've explained my theories to her, as well as where I think Al and Mike might be involved. I'm not totally convinced of any wrongdoing by Al, but there's something fishy for sure with

Mike regarding the London Fog Gang, and I'm going to find out what it is.

"Hate to cut this short," I tell her, "but my mom is about to tip Gayle and Marie off, if she hasn't already." I'm praying Meg gets her out of there, and they're both okay, but since I haven't ruled out their involvement with the death of Evelyn Jacoby, I'm a little panicked.

"They could go on the run again before you blink." My gut tightens even more at the thought. "I'm on my way to try and contain the situation, but I strongly suggest you round them up before you bring Al and Mike in for questioning. If you can figure out the link between the four, this tangled mess of threads will unravel."

She sighs. "I'll see what I can do. Don't let her blow this for us, Charlie."

We disconnect, and a part of me hopes she's bringing backup. I instruct Siri to send Matt a response. *Protect them. On my way. Ten minutes out.*

I break land speed records, pulling up and noting Matt's Mustang as well as another car parked there. Al's.

Are they all inside? It's a flippin' party, I guess. I haven't heard anything further from him or Meg on my way here, and as I climb out, I get the answer to my question—a gun goes off at Gayle's house.

My blood runs cold and my first instinct is to rush in. The former agent in me, pauses, assessing the situation and my options in rapid fire sequence. I grab my gun from my purse and eye the property as I dial 911. When the operator answers, all I say is, "There's been a shooting," and rattle off the address.

In my favorite Kate Spade white shirt and burgundy linen skirt, I have nowhere to hide my gun, so I don't. The front door is ajar, but I weigh the odds of leaving myself exposed using that entrance. My instincts tell me to find a different way.

Their garage door is halfway up—possibly to allow heat to

escape. Folks around here do that all the time. I see the not-so-hidden cameras Gayle just installed and figure he and Marie are distracted enough not to notice if I sneak under the metal entrance.

Unfortunately, it requires getting on my hands and knees. Kicking off my heels, I crawl under as quickly as I can, considering my attire. My gaze goes to the door I noted the night of our break-in.

I can hear a woman yelling. A sob and a plea.

I'm positive it leads to the kitchen and the knob is cool, even in the hot garage, under my fingers.

Ear to the door panel, I listen to the continuing half-yelling, half-sobbing. Definitely Marie.

Turning the metal ever so slowly, I find, to my great relief, it's unlocked. Inch by inch, I ease it open, seeing the side of a fridge, late '80s blue and white linoleum, geese on a wallpaper border over the sink.

I don't have time to assess the rest, a line of people along the far wall. Matt, Meg, Al, and Mom. Gayle is nowhere to be seen but Marie has her back to me. She's waving a gun and her anger has leveled up, the crying seeping away.

Ice fills my veins again. I can't breathe.

The brunt of her anger seems directed at Al, a string of healthy curses labeling him in very creative ways. "I hate you," she snarls at him. "You ruined my life!"

Four sets of eyes jerk to me as I widen the opening, but Marie is too busy with her caterwauling about money and Evelyn and years of living as someone else, to notice.

Al and Matt's gazes return to her, pretending I'm not there. I put a finger to my lips so Mom and Meg realize I have a plan to save them.

I'm not exactly sure what that is, but my training is a beautiful thing. It works better when I don't overthink the details and let my natural instincts kick in.

On silent, bare feet, I sneak behind Marie, lifting the butt of my gun to rap the back of her head. Just as I'm about to bring it down, Gayle appears, carrying two suitcases.

"I grabbed what I could." His hard eyes are leveled on Al and not at her. "Let's..."

He's heading toward the door where I'm standing, to reach the getaway car, and now he shifts his eyes.

Game over.

"Behind you!" he yells.

Before I can strike her, Marie whips around, gun pointed at my face. My weapon is already raised, but the wrong end is aimed at her. Still, hoping to capitalize on the confusion, I yell, "Drop it!"

Her bottom lip trembles, and so does the hand holding the gun.

"Shoot her," Gayle says under his breath. "We've got to get out of here. Now."

"You don 't want to do that." I stay immobile, hoping not to set her off. I want to keep her attention on me and away from the others, along with Gayle, giving Matt—and I hope, Al—an opening to jump our two felons. "The FBI is already on the way, Marie. Your time on the run is over. Put the gun down."

I see the instant her expression changes, see her shaking hand steady. As Gayle steps closer to her, once again urging her to shoot me, two things happen at once—Al strikes out and punches him, knocking him sideways, and Marie says, "You bitch."

With my instincts fully in control, I'm quicker than her trigger finger, and as the gun goes off, I dive sideways.

Matt tackles Marie, knocking her into the refrigerator and snatching the gun away. Al and Gayle wrestle behind them, Al administering another punch that leaves Gayle unconscious. Matt snags plastic zip ties from a back pocket and trusses up Marie with several swift moves.

Her caterwauling starts all over again. Gayle blinks his eyes open as Matt hands Al another for his wrists.

I wheel around to my mom and sister. "Is everyone okay?" I ask over the ear-grating noise.

"Oh Charlie." Meg grips me hard in a tight hug. "We're fine."

Sirens sound in the distance, and I heave a sigh of relief. I glance at Mom and see she's frozen in place, watching the two men shift Gayle and Marie to the sink cabinet, forcing them to sit side-by-side. Then she stalks over and slaps Marie, knocking her into Gayle.

"You're the bitch," she says, voice jerky. She raises a hand to deliver another blow. "You ever threaten one of my daughters again, I'll wipe the deck with you."

I snag her raised hand, and Meg and I, together, draw her into the living room. We exchange hugs, and as the police, then Taylor and several FBI agents, pull up, we sag down on the sofa, a blue tweed that's as stuck in the past as our felons have been.

With great satisfaction, Mom watches as Gayle and his girl-friend are led out in handcuffs.

Taylor lets me know she's bringing Al in. He's not under arrest—yet—but she does want to question him. He gives all three of us a hang-dog look. Mom tells him everything'll be okay.

I hope it will.

As we stand on the front porch and watch the cars pulling away, Gayle glares at us from the backseat of a cruiser. I put my arm around Mom's shoulders.

Meg encircles her waist from the other side, and the three of us share a moment as we watch our investigation come to a satisfying end.

26

Meg

*I*t's late.

Well, not late-late, but by nine, I should be at one of our respective homes, snuggled up to Jerome.

Instead, I'm seated on the stool in my office studying a cast of a skull delivered three hours ago by a sheriff from New Jersey.

Another cold case. Another victim needing our services.

I'm okay with it. Excited even. It's time for me to stop chasing creepy neighbors and get my hands back into clay. All this running around is Charlie's deal. Not mine.

The reconstructions are important. A few months ago, I'd stay up all night with this. Now, for the first time, I'm lacking the desperation to push beyond my emotional limits.

I have Jerome now. A positive outlet that allows me to enjoy the present and, well, just being. Standing still and breathing.

It's a good life.

"Hey."

I turn to the door where Charlie stands. After our return from Mom's, she changed into the extra pair of jeans and a short-sleeved pullover she keeps in her office. Her feet are bare.

"No shoes, huh?"

She smiles. "Accidentally left them at Gayle's. Mom's got them." She gestures to the skull. "What do you think?"

I know what she's asking. My sister, as hard-nosed as she is, has a little desperation inside her, too. She wants to solve cases as much as I do.

"Female," I say. "Or maybe a child. I'm not far enough into it. She's been sitting in a morgue for twenty years."

Charlie's low whistle fills the room. "Have you named her?"

She often lectures me about getting too attached to cold cases. My penchant for naming the victims—in Charlie's opinion—is a sure sign.

"Not yet." I smile ruefully, unwilling to let her have any satisfaction. "I have ideas, though."

"I'm sure you do. Can you take a break? Taylor just called. She's coming over with Matt. She has info for us. About Gayle."

A chime sounds from the back door opening and a second later Matt calls out.

"We're in Meg's office," Charlie responds.

Matt appears, Taylor beside him. He's dressed casually in jeans and a T-shirt while Taylor's suit, although lovely, carries wrinkles and creases befitting an extremely long day.

"Well," she says, "we'd better go to the conference room. It's a humdinger."

At that, I snort. Weren't they all lately?

Gently, I run my hand over the top of the skull mounted on a stand in front of me. "Be right back. Don't go anywhere."

"Swear to God, Meg," Charlie says. "Sometimes you are downright weird."

This is news to her?

I follow them to where Charlie has slapped on the overhead light and we take our seats. Charlie at the end and Matt and I on either side with Taylor beside him. The arrangement has started to become the norm. Obviously, Taylor has spent far too much time here recently.

Charlie sets her right hand down and gently drums her fingers. "What'd you find out?"

"Gayle and Marie," Taylor says. "Jan VanHolmes and Mary Rowlands. As you know, they're fugitives. Currently using identities they stole from two people who died in the fifties."

Nothing about that was a surprise. I've learned that folks living off the grid often steal names from the deceased. It's shockingly easy—even with today's security—to obtain a copy of a birth certificate and turn it into a new life. "Was Marie in the London Fog Gang?"

"Outside of being the girlfriend of member Henry Dieder? No. He was killed in the raid, along with Sven. She heard from Gayle the takedown had gone bad. He'd called, warning her the feds would be knocking on the door anytime."

"She ran," I say.

Taylor gives a definitive nod. "She did. Svenson hid the money under a loose floorboard in their apartment. Evelyn found it one day while cleaning, and when Henry and Marie broke up for a stint—they did that a lot, from Marie's confession—Marie stayed with her. Evelyn showed her the stash."

"And they left it there?" I ask.

"Yep. Evelyn was afraid if Sven knew she'd discovered it, he'd move it. And Marie? Not stupid. She and Evelyn knew if the relationship ever went bad, Evelyn needed to know where it was. Just in case. When Evelyn's so-called beloved died, she grabbed the money and ran. Marie went with her. They paid Gayle to set them up with fake identities and went their separate ways."

I take a second to ponder this. If Gayle and Marie separated, why were they living together?

Charlie gives Taylor her puzzled face. "How does Al play into this? Based on what Meg told me about him showing up at Gayle's earlier, they seemed to know each other."

"This is where it gets good," Matt says.

Taylor makes a warning noise in the back of her throat. She doesn't want him to give away the punchline. It's hers. "Turns out, Al, after so many years with the Bureau built a nice little network of informants that helped him close cases fast." Taylor rolls her hand. "It's no secret they use paid informants. Gayle was one of Al's. Gayle, an accomplished forger, was originally busted on a check scam that involved wire fraud. Facing federal charges, he made a deal and started snitching on his buddies in the London Fog Gang. He was their driver."

"I knew it," Charlie says.

My mind drifts back to mom's curiosity with Gayle. From the first weeks of his moving in, her instincts had flared. She may have been wrong about him being a serial killer, but she'd nailed him as having something to hide. And we teased her about it.

Shame mounts inside me. She's due a whopping apology. Along with a firm pat on the back for being an excellent investigator.

I peer at Charlie. "Mom was right. All this time, we thought she was nuts."

"She is a little, and he's not a serial killer, technically, but I owe her an apology."

I look at Taylor. "I don't understand how Gayle got away from the FBI? Why weren't they looking for him?"

"They were. At least Al was. His partner, though? After Al recruited Gayle, Grenado strong-armed him. Took a little side money when he needed it. The deal was, he'd handle the

Bureau and keep Gayle out of prison and Gayle would continue to snitch on the gang."

"That SOB." I shake my head. "He was profiting from the robberies and making himself look good by having an informant."

"Unfortunately, Baez looked the other way more times than not."

"A good partner who had his back," Charlie says.

Taylor shrugs. "There was an internal investigation, but it never went anywhere."

Charlie drums her fingers again. "A little bird told me about it." She doesn't say JJ, refusing to out him to Taylor, but we all know who she's talking about. "The Bureau kept it quiet, so it wouldn't become public that one of their own was on the take."

"From what Gayle told us," Taylor says, "Grenado caught up with him the night of the takedown. Gayle handed him thirty grand and warned him to leave him be or he'd take him down. Once a snitch, always a snitch, I suppose."

"Mike let him go," Charlie says. "He got the money and just let him walk."

That about sums it up. "Mary/Marie goes one way, Gayle the other, Evelyn a third, but they agree to stay in touch periodically in case one of them gets into trouble. Fast forward six months and Mary is living in North Carolina. She's on a day trip exploring the area and runs into Evelyn, who is now born again."

"Seriously?" I ask. "She's living on money obtained in bank robberies. How is that the good Christian thing to do?"

Taylor holds a hand up. "It gets better. Evelyn invites Mary to her hotel room for tea where she tries to convince her to find the Lord. Claims she's been struggling, trying to decide what to do with the money because—as you say—it's not the Christian thing. Suddenly, she's inspired. Seeing Mary has enlightened her. According to Mary/Marie, she's twirling around the room, elated that the Lord has sent her a sign."

"What sign?" Charlie wants to know.

"Mary, of course. Her showing up is a sign that she—and by extension Marie—should turn themselves in. Be free of the ill-gotten money that'll surely send them to hell."

Speechless, I glance at Charlie.

"This new, holy-rolling Evelyn," Taylor continues, "spooks Marie. She has no interest in turning herself in. She's quite happy risking a stint in hell. And she doesn't trust that God-fearing Ev might not snitch on her whereabouts."

Matt makes a humming noise. "Marie still has all the bank robbery money."

"Damn," Charlie says.

Taylor gives a succinct nod. "Ev continues haranguing Marie and, according to Marie, she starts wigging out. Insisting they go to the police together. She's counting on their child-hood friendship to prevail. But Mary, she's too afraid of prison. They argue and," Taylor brings her hands up to her throat, "Marie strangles her. Today, she claimed it was accidental, but whatever. She then shoved the body in a large rolling suitcase and took her right through the lobby."

If ever I needed a pot brownie, it was now. "Hang on. Marie killed her? In North Carolina?"

"Yes. She panicked."

I get all that. What shocks the hell out of me is how Marie got Evelyn's body to Whitetop Mountain in Virginia.

And then it hits me. I sit back and blow out a breath. "She called Gayle. Told him what happened and he helped her dispose of the body."

Taylor gestures as if she's ringing a bell. "Ding, ding. Give Meg her prize."

But the other two? It couldn't be a coincidence that all three were buried there. And, ohmygod. My crazy mother may have been right all along.

I lean forward, resting my hands on the table and digging my fingertips into the top. "Please, Taylor. Tell me a serial killer hasn't actually been living across the street from my parents."

"A serial killer has not been living across the street."

Thank you.

"Remember," she continues, "Evelyn's boyfriend had some twisted sexual fetishes. He liked to choke girls out during sex."

"Bastard," Charlie mutters.

"Apparently, Gayle wasn't above helping his buddy dump a couple of bodies."

"Bastards, plural," Charlie says. "So, Marie calls Gayle in a panic and Gayle tells her he knows a place."

Taylor rests her index finger on her nose. "They bury Evelyn near the other two, so it looks like one person buried them all."

One person did bury them all.

He just wasn't the killer.

Two pot brownies tonight.

At least.

I look at Charlie, the full weight of what my mother had gotten herself into now hitting me. "Mom could've gotten killed. Just like Evelyn."

Charlie nods. "Imagine Al's surprise when Mom goes to his cold case group asking for help with her quirky neighbor." Charlie looks at Taylor. "All this time, Al's been working with her and he's known exactly who Gayle is."

"Yep. He's been trying to protect your mom, afraid Grenado would get wind of it. What with Gayle threatening to take him down if he ever saw him again. Al's been keeping an eye on Gayle and getting intel from your mother. While trying to figure out how to turn in his ex-partner and keep your mother safe."

My mother. The rock star.

"We have to tell Mom," I say to Charlie. "It'll break her heart about Al, but she's...amazing. Her hard work brought these people down."

27

Charlie

I host Sunday lunch this week with Meg and Jerome, JJ, Mom and Dad, and we've added Taylor and Matt.

The men are on the patio, JJ grilling and fending off questions from my dad regarding a run for office. He and I still haven't discussed this idea, but I know it's far in the future, if at all.

Jerome is, surprisingly, holding his own on sports and politics with Matt. They seem to be getting along quite well. I suspect Jerome will be around permanently, so it's a good thing.

Taylor is showing off her new engagement ring, thanks to Matt, who finally went shopping with Meg and landed the perfect diamond. We've made all the appropriate noises, Meg keeping her input a secret and giving Matt all the glory at choosing a ring Taylor adores.

The three of us putter around the kitchen, getting together

some of the side dishes and drinks. Mom is in the dining room laying out plates and silverware.

Meg has been invited to speak at a forensic conference in the fall on her techniques for rebuilding the dead. She's already making notes and practicing her speech.

The A/C is finally fixed, and I've decided to give Haley a few more responsibilities. She has some interest in doing investigative work, and I'm hiring a friend of Matt's part-time to help with the more mundane tasks, such as surveillance, which Matt and I both hate. Mom's two friends from the CSCC group have also offered to help us catch up with paperwork.

My car is totaled and I've already started scanning online sites to replace it when the insurance check arrives. Taylor managed to get a confession out of that scumbag, Mike, that he was the one who shot at me. I'm considering calling Jackie DelRay for a referral on a civil attorney so I can sue his ass.

Mom returns, grabbing a handful of napkins to take back. She's slightly depressed, the case that consumed her for nearly twenty years is solved. Meg and I sat her down and brought her up to speed earlier, and she was both satisfied and slightly at a loss. What comes next? The Citizens Solving Cold Cases is disbanding, talking about starting a new group and making her their president, but she doesn't seem all that excited about it.

JJ and Dad bring in trays of grilled meat and veggies and everyone takes their time sitting at the dining room table. It's nice when it gets to be used for its real purpose, instead of my second office, scattered with files and my laptop. Casual conversation fills the air. We're talking and laughing, enjoying a relaxing get together. I feel blessed to have all these people in my life.

After we snag our food and dig in, a comfortable silence falls. Mom is at one end, Dad the other. JJ's across from me, Meg and Jerome next to him. Taylor and Matt are on my right.

Even though it's quiet, Mom suddenly clinks her silverware against her water glass to get our attention.

"As you all know, we've resolved the Gayle case. I just want to thank Charlie and Meg, and you, Matt,"—her gaze goes to him and she smiles—"for helping me bring him to justice."

In unison we raise our glasses to salute her, but Mom isn't done. She accepts the congratulations, then makes an announcement. "Now that I've finished up that investigation, I'm looking for employment."

Her gaze lands on me, and then Meg, a question. An invitation.

A boatload of hope.

No one knows her better than Meg, and she anticipated this —that mom needed a new hobby, a new focus. We discussed it, even bringing Dad in on it secretly, but we do not expect what comes next.

Mom's smile is wide. "I want to work for Schock Investigations."

Silence falls like an ax, this time startled, weighted.

All eyes swing to me.

I need to handle this carefully. Meg's face tells me she's torn between wanting to give Mom a new purpose, and knowing if she works for us, she'll drive us to drink more than we already do.

Still, her skills, she's proven, are top-notch. The Schock women are quite a force.

I clear my throat and act as though I need a sip of water before I can answer, stalling. I can't say yes, but I can't say no either. I search for some kind of happy medium, wondering how I always ends up on the spot at these Sunday lunches.

"We can always use a researcher," I say, choosing my words carefully. Meg sees where I'm going with this and nods encouragement. "Your friends are assisting with paperwork. You could manage them for us."

"You can run background checks and do follow-ups with clients," she adds. "It'll be perfect, because you can work from home, part-time, and just come to the office for our Monday morning meetings. You can get new assignments and bring us up to speed on your research."

Her eyes light up, and I know she's already considering the types of cases she can stick her nose in.

Dad, being Dad, tries to help us out. "Why do you want to go back to work, honey? We talked about buying an RV and traveling the country. I thought we were going to do that, since you don't have to keep an eye on the neighbors anymore."

He gives her a wink.

Mom hesitates, her smile fading slightly. "That's true, but..."

"As long as you have wi-fi, we can email the information." There has to be a way to make this work. "You can handle research on the road. Win-win."

Her fingers play with her glass, twirling it slowly. "I don't have the computer skills like you gals, though."

Matt speaks up. "Our friend, Teeg, can help. He'll have you up and running in no time."

Teeg is a hacker for Justice Greystone and his team. I'm pretty sure his skills are not exactly what I want my mother to learn, but on the other hand...

Before I can steer the conversation in a different direction, the doorbell rings. JJ offers to get it, but I wave him off, tossing my napkin on the table. "I've got it."

I'm quite dumbfounded to find Al on the doorstep. He looks at me sheepishly, hands folded in front of him, head tilted down. "I don't mean to intrude," he says. "But I needed to apologize to all of you, and especially—"

"Alfonzo?" Mom is at my side. She reaches out toward him, and he takes her hand. "Are you okay?"

He nods and releases her, keeping his spot, a respectful distance. "I'm still facing charges for covering up my former partner's illegal acts, but I'm free for now. I'm sure Charlie and Meg told you about... Well, everything. I wanted to say I'm sorry for lying to you, Helen. I was in a tough spot, trying to keep you safe while not disclosing my...acquaintance...with Gayle."

"Al," Mom says, "I'll admit, I was surprised, but I can see where you'd be conflicted. I do appreciate you coming, though."

He reaches into his back pocket and pulls out a business card to hand to her. "I wanted to give you this."

I cock my head to read over Mom's shoulder. Mary Goldstein, Crime Desk, D.C. Investigative Journal.

Mom glances at me and back to the name. We both look at Al.

He points at the card. "A contact of mine. She'd like to talk to you about their monthly cold case articles, see if you'd be interested in researching and writing for them."

It's a tabloid, but a fairly respected one. Most of their reporting is online, but they also put out special print editions. Haley loves them.

The reporter instinct in my mother is strong, combined with her natural investigative abilities, and this is right up her alley. Still, she looks as gobsmacked as I am. "Why, I'd be thrilled, but surely there are more qualified people than me."

Al's smile is sad, but at the same time, not. I can tell he really does care for her, and I have the feeling if he ends up in prison for his misdeeds, he'll have a regular visitor. "No one is a better fit than you."

He says goodbye and Mom, blushing, returns to the dining room. I follow noting how unusually quiet she is again as she fingers the card.

Dad asks who was at the door, Mom resumes her seat and beams. "Looks like I won't be working for Meg and Charlie. I have a new job as a reporter again."

She shows off Goldstein's card, and it gets passed around. No one comments about the sensationalism the journal often depends on for its popularity. This is Washington D.C., after all.

But I sure hope this person comes through for Mom, and for me and Meg, too.

As Mom chatters excitedly about this potential new job, and how she might work for them and Schock Investigations, I exchange a glance with my sister.

Meg smiles, reading my mind, like always, before she passes the potato salad to Jerome. He plops a spoonful on her plate, and she leans in to him, her happiness palpable.

Dad reaches over and squeezes my hand briefly, as if letting me know he's proud of me. For solving the case with Meg, or offering Mom a job? Maybe both. It doesn't matter; I return it.

Across the table, JJ catches my eye. He winks. I slide my toes under his pant leg in response. We have plans for each other later, after everyone leaves, and the smoldering look he gives me makes my toes curl.

Those unicorn pajamas won't be needed tonight.

My family is safe, my friends happy. Some days the good guys win, I tell myself.

And this is one of those days.

ABOUT THE AUTHORS

USA TODAY bestselling Author Misty Evans has published over fifty novels and writes romantic suspense, urban fantasy, and paranormal romance. Under her pen name, Nyx Halliwell, she also writes small-town cozy mysteries.

When not reading or writing, she enjoys music, movies, and hanging out with her husband, twin sons, and three spoiled rescue dogs. Get your free story and sign up for her newsletter at www.readmistyevans.com. Like her author page on Facebook or follow her on Twitter.

Adrienne Giordano is a *USA Today* bestselling author of over twenty-five romantic suspense and mystery novels. She is a Jersey girl at heart, but now lives in the Midwest with her ultimate supporter of a husband, sports-obsessed son and Elliot, a snuggle-happy rescue. Having grown up near the ocean, Adrienne enjoys paddleboarding, a nice float in a kayak and lounging on the beach with a good book. For more information on Adrienne's books, please visit http://www.AdrienneGiordano.com.

Adrienne can also be found on Facebook at http://www.facebook.com/AdrienneGiordanoAuthor, Twitter at http://twitter.com/AdriennGiordano and Goodreads at http://www.goodreads.com/AdrienneGiordano. For information on Adrienne's Facebook reader group go to https://www.facebook.com/groups/AdrienneGiordanoReaderGroup

Dear reader,

Thank you for reading this book. We hope you enjoyed it! If you did, please help others find it by leaving a review at Goodreads or your favorite retailer. Even a few sentences about what you loved about the book will be extremely appreciated!!

Thank you!

Misty & Adrienne

BOOKS BY ADRIENNE GIORDANO

JUSTICE TEAM SERIES w/MISTY EVANS
Stealing Justice
Cheating Justice
Holiday Justice
Exposing Justice
Undercover Justice
Protecting Justice
Missing Justice
Defending Justice

SCHOCK SISTERS MYSTERY SERIES w/Misty Evans
1st Shock
2nd Strike
3rd Tango

THE LUCIE RIZZO MYSTERY SERIES
Dog Collar Crime
Knocked Off
Limbo (novella)
Boosted

Books by Adrienne Giordano

Whacked
Cooked
Incognito

PRIVATE PROTECTOR SERIES
Risking Trust
Man Law
A Just Deception
Negotiating Point
Relentless Pursuit
Opposing Forces

HARLEQUIN INTRIGUES
The Prosecutor
The Defender
The Marshal
The Detective
The Rebel

JUSTIFIABLE CAUSE SERIES
The Chase
The Evasion
The Capture

CASINO FORTUNA SERIES
Deadly Odds

**STEELE RIDGE SERIES w/KELSEY BROWNING
& TRACEY DEVLYN**
Steele Ridge: The Beginning
Going Hard (Kelsey Browning)
Living Fast (Adrienne Giordano)
Loving Deep (Tracey Devlyn)
Breaking Free (Adrienne Giordano)

Roaming Wild (Tracey Devlyn)
Stripping Bare (Kelsey Browning)

STEELE RIDGE SERIES: The Kingstons w/KELSEY BROWNING & TRACEY DEVLYN
Craving HEAT (Adrienne Giordano)
Tasting FIRE (Kelsey Browning)
Searing NEED (Tracey Devlyn)
Striking EDGE (Kelsey Browning)
Burning ACHE (Adrienne Giordano)

BOOKS BY MISTY EVANS

The Justice Team Series (with Adrienne Giordano)

Stealing Justice

Cheating Justice

Holiday Justice

Exposing Justice

Undercover Justice

Protecting Justice

Missing Justice

Defending Justice

SCHOCK SISTERS MYSTERY SERIES w/Adrienne Giordano

1st Shock

2nd Strike

3rd Tango

SEALS of Shadow Force Series: Spy Division

Man Hunt

Man Killer

Man Down

SEALs of Shadow Force Series

Fatal Truth

Fatal Honor

Fatal Courage

Fatal Love

Fatal Vision

Fatal Thrill

Risk

The SCVC Taskforce Series

Deadly Pursuit

Deadly Deception

Deadly Force

Deadly Intent

Deadly Affair, A SCVC Taskforce novella

Deadly Attraction

Deadly Secrets

Deadly Holiday, A SCVC Taskforce novella

Deadly Target

Deadly Rescue

Deadly Bounty (coming January 2020)

The Super Agent Series

Operation Sheba

Operation Paris

Operation Proof of Life

Operation Lost Princess (formerly The Blood Code, releasing
February 2020)

The Secret Ingredient Culinary Mystery Series

The Secret Ingredient, A Culinary Romantic Mystery with Bonus Recipes

The Secret Life of Cranberry Sauce, A Secret Ingredient Holiday Novella

CPSIA information can be obtained
at www.ICGtesting.com
Printed in the USA
LVHW100140270320
651357LV00006B/57